I0634134

The Communist Manifesto

A Revolutionary Fairy Tale

Karlyn Borysenko

RED MENACE PRESS

Copyright © 2025 Karlyn Borysenko
All rights reserved.

No part of this book may be reproduced, stored in a retrieval system, or trans-
mitted in any form or by any means—electronic, mechanical, photocopying,
recording, or otherwise—without the prior written permission of the publisher,
except in the case of brief quotations embodied in critical articles or reviews.

This is a work of fiction. Names, characters, places, and incidents are products
of the author's imagination or are used fictitiously. Any resemblance to actual
events, locales, or persons, living or dead, is entirely coincidental.

Published by
Red Menace Press
RedMenacePress.com

For permissions and inquiries, contact:
contact@redmenacepress.com

CONTENTS

DEDICATION

To John Morgan, the master of the fan fiction.

WARNING

Fairy tales were never meant to be comforting.

They were brutal, bloody warnings
whispered through the ages
to keep people from wandering into darkness.

This book is violent, cruel,
and deeply uncomfortable.

But it is the truth.

Read at your own risk.

ACT I

THE ENCHANTED CHAINS

THE BRAND SIZZLED AGAINST Eliza Shaw's hand, her flesh yielding to the Merchant King's crown with a hiss that seemed to echo through the Gray Quarter. The Palace Guard pressed harder than necessary, ensuring the mark would last.

Moments earlier, the Scale Master had declared "Insufficient!" after weighing her week's earnings with barely a glance. Rain plastered his uniform to his shoulders, but his voice remained dry as dust.

"But that's everything," Eliza had whispered, pushing a strand of her copper-brown hair away from her face. "The Mill reduced our—"

"Hand," interrupted the third Guard, who had already been reaching for the metal brand heating in a small brazier attached to the wagon.

Now, as the searing pain spread through her palm, Eliza's thoughts turned to her daughter. How would she explain to Lily that their water rations would be reduced? How would she keep the fever at bay without enough clean water?

"Water rations reduced for three days," the ledger Guard announced, already turning toward the next dwelling, already forgetting her existence.

Pain was the punctuation at the end of a familiar sentence in the Kingdom of Laboria.

***

Once upon a time, in the prosperous yet peculiar Kingdom of Laboria, there existed two lands within one border. Not different realms on any map you'd find in the Royal Cartographer's dusty archives, but territories as distinct as dream and nightmare. Ask any child with dirt-smudged cheeks and eyes too old for their years, and they'd point exactly where one ended and the other began.

The border smelled of desperation and tasted of ash. You knew the moment you'd crossed it.

In the northern hills stood Palace Heights, where mansions stretched their spires toward the sun like greedy fingers trying to claim the very sky as private property. The Merchant King's palace dominated the landscape, a monument to excess built by hands that could never hope to enter it except as servants. From its highest tower, the King himself often surveyed his domain through a golden spyglass, counting the plumes of colored smoke from the Mills as others might count jewels.

"Production appears steady today," he would observe to his chief advisor, a thin man whose spectacles gleamed as coldly as his calculations. "Has the Northern Mill reached its new quota?"

"Not yet, Your Prosperity," the advisor would reply, consulting his meticulous ledgers. "But we've reduced rations by fifteen percent. Production should increase accordingly by week's end."

"Excellent," the King would nod, stroking his beard adorned with golden threads and tiny jewels. "Suffering has always been our most reliable motivator."

The Merchant King and his bloated Royal Council lived in such obscene splendor that gardeners spent sixteen-hour days training flowers to bloom in patterns spelling out family crests. Their children wore clothes woven from moonbeams and butterfly whispers. They dined on feasts so elaborate that entire courses existed solely to cleanse one's palate for the next indulgence, served on plates that cost more than a Gray Quarter family would earn in three lifetimes. Their greatest hardship was deciding which of their seventeen ballrooms might best suit the evening's festivities, or whether the east wing fountains should flow with wine or perfumed water for Tuesday's garden soiree.

Beyond the golden gates and the rigid hedge mazes of Palace Heights lay the Gray Quarter, where perfection crumbled into neglect. Here, the sun seemed reluctant, like a shy lover, to shed its warmth with the same enthusiasm.

The cobblestones had forgotten how to remain level, sitting crooked like the backs of those who walked them daily.

In cramped cottages with perpetually leaking roofs, the workers of Laboria rose before dawn and returned long after dusk. Their hands were calloused, maps of pain etched into flesh, whole histories of labor written in cracked skin and bent fingers.

Eliza Shaw lived in one such cottage. Its walls were so thin that winter winds played them like flutes, creating a constant melody of misery. The gaps between the boards whistled different notes depending on the direction of the wind. Sometimes a mournful requiem from the north, some-times a frantic, squealing shriek from the east. The cottage's one window had long lost any glass it might once have possessed. A scrap of cloth hung limply, a useless guardian against the elements.

At twenty-nine, Eliza's face already showed the prema-ture lines of constant worry. Green eyes that had once sparked with determination now looked tired beneath her dark lashes. Tonight, those eyes reflected fear as she knelt beside her daughter's bed, pressing a damp cloth to the child's burning forehead.

"Hush now, Lily-flower," she whispered, though the girl hadn't made a sound in hours. The silence frightened Eliza more than crying ever could.

This wasn't the life Eliza had imagined for herself. There had been a time when she had believed the Spell of Necessity herself. She had swallowed it whole, like bitter medicine.

Her father had been a skilled supervisor in the North-ern Mill, one of the few Gray Quarter residents permitted to wear the blue cap of Technical Expertise. The cap that marked him as better than most, but still far beneath the lowest Palace Heights servant. Their family had lived in the slightly better eastern edge of the Quarter, in a home with actual glass windows and a private water pump that only broke three times a year instead of monthly.

"You're fortunate, Eliza," her father often told her, his voice carrying the grinding sound of someone who had convinced himself of a comfortable lie. "The Merchant King rewards exceptional skill. Learn the loom patterns well enough, and you could earn the blue cap too."

She had believed him, studying pattern-making with monastic dedication, her fingers bleeding at night as she practiced on scraps stolen from the Mill floor. At sixteen, she had been chosen for the advanced weaving program, an honor that made her parents beam with pride. The other girls in her street had looked at her with envy tinged with resentment. A future of relative comfort seemed assured.

Then came the Mill Efficiency Decree. Supervisors like her father were suddenly deemed unnecessarily elevated laborers, their positions eliminated in favor of Noble Overseers from Palace Heights who knew nothing of the work but wore the right family crests. Her father's protests earned him reassignment to the most dangerous section of the Northern Mill. The boiler section, where men aged a year for every month they worked.

When the boiler explosion happened two months later, the official report cited worker incompetence. Never mind that he had warned of the faulty pressure valve for weeks. He had documented it, and begged for the three-copper repair that would have saved those twelve lives.

With her family's modest security vanished like morning mist, Eliza had been forced to abandon her advanced training and take any position available. At seventeen, she married Thomas, a kind young man from the Western Quarter who worked the loading docks. When Lily came a few years later, they had been happy despite their circumstances. It's always the happiness which flourishes where it shouldn't that tastes sweetest because you know it cannot last.

And it didn't. Thomas was selected for the Foreign Trade Fleet, a virtual death sentence of three-year voyages to distant kingdoms on ships barely seaworthy, with crews treated worse than the rats that infested their hulls. His last letter had arrived two years ago. The shipping office had stopped accepting her inquiries six months after that. They had threatened to report her for disruptive behavior when she'd continued asking.

Survival now consumed Eliza's every waking moment. The myth of advancement through exceptional service had died with her father. The fantasy of family security had vanished with Thomas. Only Lily remained, her single light in an ever-darkening world. And now even that light flickered dangerously as fever ravaged her daughter's tiny body.

"Mama," ten-year-old Lily whispered through cracked lips the color of faded roses. Her honey-colored hair, usually so vibrant against her fair skin, lay damp and lifeless on the pillow. "I'm so thirsty."

Eliza reached for the water cup, finding it empty. The communal pump had stopped working three days ago, and the Palace Guards now rationed water from barrels, one cupful per person per day. She had already given Lily her own ration, had watched her daughter drink it in desperate gulps that left nothing for later.

"Just a little longer, love," Eliza murmured, hiding her trembling hands in the folds of her skirt. "The medicine will help soon."

This was a lie. There was no medicine. The apothecary had turned her away that morning when she couldn't produce the five silver coins required. That was more than she earned in a month at the Mill. "The fever lily remedy comes from Palace Heights gardens," he had explained with rehearsed regret, not meeting her eyes. "Very rare. Very expensive. Nothing I can do."

The irony wasn't lost on Eliza. Her daughter, named for a common wildflower that grew in abundance beyond the kingdom's walls, would enter adolescence only to potentially die for lack of an ornamental bloom that decorated noble dinner tables.

When Eliza returned to her cottage, soaking her branded palm in their precious drinking water allotment, Lily watched with eyes too knowing for her years.

"Does it hurt bad?" she finally asked, her small face solemn in the dim light.

Eliza almost lied, then stopped herself. False comfort taught dangerous lessons. "Yes," she said simply. "But pain passes. Hunger doesn't."

Lily nodded, her eyes older than her years. "At school, they say we should be grateful. That the Mills provide for everyone according to their proper place."

Her voice took on a questioning tone. "But our place always seems to be hungry."

Eliza tensed, glancing at the thin walls as if Guards might be listening. "Be careful where you say such things. Even true observations can be dangerous."

"I know," Lily replied with a maturity that made Eliza's heart ache. "I only say the approved things at school. I save my questions for home."

They both understood that the Palace Guards would return next Sunday, and the one after that, taking more than was given, branding those who couldn't pay, a cycle as changeless as the seasons. Not because there wasn't enough in Laboria for everyone, the wagons that carried food and textiles to Palace Heights proved otherwise, but because suffering itself was the currency that kept the Merchant King's ledgers balanced.

***

Life in the Gray Quarter followed immutable patterns, as rigid as the factory shifts yet lacking any official mandate. Each morning began with the Factory Bells, enormous iron monsters that ripped workers violently from their sleep while the elegant chimes of Palace Heights barely stirred their nobles from their pleasant dreams.

The communal water pumps became the first battleground of each day. Workers lined up with dented metal buckets, watching the handles gush rusty liquid for the first dozen pulls before clearing to something drinkable. Palace

Guards supervised the larger pumps, enforcing the strict ration. One bucket per family, no exceptions.

"Next! Move along now," barked a Guard, striking his baton against the pump's stone base when anyone took too long.

The walk to the Mills formed the next ritual, a river of bent backs and downcast eyes flowing through streets deliberately designed to remind workers of their station. The cobblestones became progressively more uneven as one traveled away from Palace Heights, with cracks and holes that filled with malodorous water after each rain. No maintenance crews ever appeared to fix them, though workers regularly paid path maintenance taxes.

At the Mill gates, daily humiliations awaited. Guards conducted random loyalty inspections, forcing selected workers to empty their pockets, recite pledges to the Merchant King, or demonstrate their knowledge of proper deference protocols. Those who failed faced docked wages or worse.

"Arms out, mouth shut," a senior Guard instructed a young man who had arrived from the rural provinces just weeks earlier. The Guard performed an exaggerated search, confiscating a small carved wooden toy the worker had made for his sister. "Unauthorized crafting," the Guard announced. "Materials belong to the Mill, not to you."

The young man said nothing, having already learned that protesting such treatment only doubled the punishment. He simply adjusted his tattered cap and moved through the gate, his shoulders slumping further under invisible weights that grew heavier each day.

Inside the Mills, workers were connected to machines rather than collaborating with each other. Conversation was discouraged through a system of production quotas that left no breath for idle words. The noises, clanging metal, hissing steam, grinding gears, created a deliberate cacophony that made human voices inaudible. Some workers believed this was by design, a way to prevent dangerous ideas from spreading during working hours.

At the heart of the kingdom stood the legendary Magical Production Mills, massive structures of stone, steel, and inexplicable enchantment. Day and night, the Mills churned and hummed, belching rainbow-colored smoke into the sky. It was said that within their walls, ordinary materials were transformed into the most wondrous goods any kingdom had ever known. Silks that changed color with one's mood, carriages that required no horses, and devices that could capture a person's voice and release it months later, word for word.

The true magic of the Mills, however, lay not in their products but in their economic alchemy, the transformation of human labor into capital that workers never touched. Raw materials entered, human skill, natural resources, dreams, and emerged as commodities stripped of their humanity. A thread woven became a garment, but the hands that created it vanished from the story, rendered invisible in the final product. This invisibility was the cornerstone of Laboria's economy, the ability to separate the maker from what was made, allowing all value to flow upward.

"The Mills are the kingdom's blessing," proclaimed the Town Criers each morning. "Through their bounty, all of Laboria prospers!"

Yet, curiously, while the Mills produced ever more goods with each passing year, the tables of Gray Quarter families held ever less food. Workers crafted exquisite furniture they would never sit upon, stitched elegant garments they would never wear, and assembled delightful toys their own children would never touch.

Eliza had spent fourteen hours that day in the Eastern Mill, her fingers raw from operating the looms that wove miraculous self-warming blankets. The previous week, she had watched Palace Guards load a shipment of these blankets onto carriages bound for Palace Heights. In the Gray Quarter, three children had frozen to death during an unexpected cold snap.

One of those children had been her neighbor's son. The memory of his tiny blue-tinged face haunted her as she looked down at Lily's flushed one. Different symptoms, same disease. The plague of poverty in a kingdom of plenty.

More curious still was that few in the Gray Quarter questioned this arrangement. When stomachs growled at night, parents would simply tighten their belts and remind their children of the Spell of Necessity.

"This is simply how things must be," they would explain with resigned sighs. "The Merchant King and Royal Council manage the Mills, and we provide the labor. It has always been so, and always shall be."

Eliza had once believed this herself. But watching Lily struggle for breath, something hardened inside her. A kernel of rebellion was taking root where acceptance had once grown.

***

In Palace Heights, the nobles had a different explanation for the kingdom's arrangement, which they discussed over thirteen-course dinners.

"The prosperity dust from the Mills rises up to us, as is natural," said Lord Puffinbottom, the Minister of Justified Inequity, while delicately dabbing his lips with an embroidered napkin that cost more than a Gray Quarter family's monthly wage. "If we allowed the workers more, they would simply become lazy and ungrateful. Their suffering is, in fact, a kindness we provide."

The dining hall of Lord Puffinbottom's manor sprawled larger than the entire communal square of the Gray Quarter's western section. Crystal chandeliers hung from thirty-foot ceilings, each containing more candles than a worker's family would use in a year. The table itself was a masterpiece of conspicuous excess, forty feet of polished mahogany inlaid with mother-of-pearl patterns depicting the natural order. Nobles above, workers below, all arranged in a harmonious hierarchy that the dinner guests found most agreeable.

Each Noble House sent representatives to these weekly governance dinners, where the kingdom's policies were determined between the fish and meat courses. Tonight's gathering was particularly well-attended, as the Merchant

King had mentioned productivity concerns in his quarterly address.

"I've found that hunger is the most effective management tool," said Baron Goldcrest, the Royal Overseer of Northern Production. "Last month, we reduced rations in the ore processing division by thirty percent. Output increased by twelve percent within a week."

"Marvelous efficiency," nodded Countess Silverchain, the Minister of Labor Distribution. "Though I've discovered that hope can be equally motivating when properly manipulated. We've introduced a 'Premium Worker' designation in the textile division. Workers who exceed their quotas by fifty percent receive a green armband and an extra bread ration once a month."

"And how many achieve this designation?" asked Lord Puffinbottom, amused.

"That's the beauty of it," Silverchain smiled, accepting a glass of wine from a servant. "We set the quotas just high enough that fewer than one percent can physically achieve them, regardless of effort. But they all work themselves to exhaustion trying. It costs us a few extra bread loaves while extracting thousands of additional labor hours."

The table erupted in appreciative laughter as servants brought in the fourth course, a delicate arrangement of imported fruits carved to resemble woodland creatures. The Countess's nine-year-old daughter clapped with delight.

"Mother, look! The little apple bird is so perfect! Can I have the artisan make one for my birthday celebration?"

"The carver isn't an artisan, darling," Silverchain corrected gently. "Just a Gray Quarter knife-worker. But yes, we'll have a hundred made for your party. They're really quite affordable when you calculate by piece rather than by worker."

As the nobles discussed the upcoming social season, comparing planned galas and festivals, none seemed aware of the irony in their earlier conversation. The very productivity they celebrated was measured in how efficiently they could extract labor while returning as little as possible to those who produced their wealth. This wasn't a side effect of their system, it was its central feature, deliberately designed and constantly refined.

***

Marcus Wheeler had been a fixture in the Eastern Mill for as long as Eliza could remember. Unlike many who kept their heads down and accepted their lot, Marcus maintained a stubborn belief that reasonable requests, properly submitted, might lead to modest improvements. A skilled mechanical operator with twenty years' experience, he had gained a measure of quiet respect even from some lower-level supervisors. His hands, strong yet precise, could repair complex machinery that baffled Noble Overseers, making him valuable enough that minor acts of defiance were sometimes overlooked.

When three children lost fingers in the dangerous cutting machines in a single month, and a fourth, a girl of just nine, lost her life, something in Marcus hardened into resolve. He was a father himself, with two daughters who would soon be old enough for Mill work. The dead child could have been his own.

His petition had been simple. Children under twelve should be limited to eight-hour shifts instead of fourteen, with at least one meal provided. As Eastern Mill's production quotas increased and adult workers collapsed from exhaustion, more children were being assigned to dangerous machinery. The request was modest, carefully worded to avoid any hint of challenge to the Merchant King's authority.

The petition journey began at the Mill's Administrative Office, where the clerk required all documents to be submitted in triplicate, written on official petition paper that cost two days' wages per sheet. Each submission required a different colored ink, available only from licensed Palace Heights stationers.

"Form D-12 is incomplete," the clerk informed Marcus after making him wait three hours. "Section 14, Paragraph C requires the exact weight of production loss anticipated from reduced child labor hours, calculated to two decimal places and verified by a licensed Efficiency Accountant."

The Efficiency Accountant, Marcus discovered, charged consulting fees equivalent to a month's wages and required payment in advance. After scraping together the money from fellow workers, Marcus returned with the completed documents, only to be told. "Petition regulations were updated yesterday. All calculations must now use the new Royal Productivity Formulas. Previous submissions are invalid."

This cycle repeated for months. When Marcus finally secured all the proper forms, signatures, and validations, he

was permitted to present his petition to the District Griev-
ance Committee, three mid-level nobles who held court for
precisely one hour each month.

"Petition 47-D-238 denied," announced the Committee
Chairman after a thirty-second review. "Insufficient economic justification for policy modification. Next petitioner."

"But the children are dying," Marcus protested, breaking
protocol by speaking after the ruling.

The Chairman signaled to the Palace Guards at the door.
"Petitioner is exhibiting signs of Emotional Decision Contamination, a violation of Petition Code 5-J. Remove him and
record the violation in his employment file."

As the Guards dragged him from the chamber, Marcus caught sight of a document on the Chairman's desk.
A pre-printed form with "PETITION DENIED" stamped
across it, lacking only the specific petition number. He realized then that the outcome had been determined before he
had even entered the room. The message was unmistakable.
The system allowed the appearance of redress without the
possibility of actual change.

Three days later, they came for him at dusk.

Eliza was returning from her shift when she saw the
Palace Guards surrounding his small dwelling. His wife
Mara's scream cut through the evening air, a sound so raw
it made people turn away. Their daughters watched from
the doorway, the younger one clutching a worn doll whose
button eyes seemed more alive than the child's frozen face.

"Citizen Marcus Wheeler stands accused of seditious
speech against His Prosperity," announced the Guard Cap-

tain to the neighbors who had gathered, some from duty, others from the terrible human instinct to witness suffering. "The punishment is the Pits."

The whisper that ran through the crowd held more fear than Eliza had heard in a single word before. The Reminder Pits. Everyone knew of them. They were the holes beyond the Northern Mill, deep enough to stand in but not lie down, exposed to sun and rain and the eyes of passing workers, a brutal reminder in the cost of speaking truth.

"What did he say?" someone dared to ask.

The Captain's smile was thin. "The accused stated that 'The King eats our children's bread' after observing a grain wagon departing from the Mill where three children had collapsed from hunger that morning."

Eliza remembered those children, how still they had lain on the Mill floor and how slowly the foreman had walked to investigate, as though their small bodies were merely inconvenient obstacles to production.

The next morning, Guards diverted all workers past the Pits on their way to shifts. A dozen holes had been dug in the hard clay, each just large enough for a standing person, each deep enough that only the heads and shoulders of the occupants were visible. Marcus occupied the center pit, the night's rain still dripping from his hair, his eyes already distant.

Above each pit stood a sign detailing the prisoner's crime. Above Marcus, it read "I questioned the King's right to the fruits of production."

For three days it rained. On the fourth day, the sun returned with vicious strength. Workers were still required to pass the Pits, to see Marcus's lips crack with thirst, to witness his daughters standing at the perimeter, not permitted to approach but made to watch.

On the fifth day, Marcus's pit stood empty.

No one asked what had happened to him. When his family was evicted for "failure to maintain productivity during bereavement," no neighbors offered shelter. When his youngest daughter collapsed from pneumonia the following week, with no father to provide for medicine, the Town Crier noted only that "Gray Quarter efficiency has improved through natural reduction of dependent population."

Eliza understood then that the Merchant King's genius lay not in the punishment itself but in making witnesses complicit through their silence, teaching that to care for another was to risk becoming like them. Fear severed community more effectively than any Guard's sword.

What haunted her most was how ordinary it all seemed the following week.

The Mills continued.

The wagons rolled.

The Palace Guards collected their tithes.

As though Marcus had never existed, as though his daughters' grief was as insignificant as rain on cobblestones.

This, too, was by design. Not just the suffering of the defiant, but the erasure that followed.

In Laboria, to be forgotten was the final punishment.

***

Throughout the Gray Quarter, strange whispers had begun to circulate. They were carried first by a figure known only as the Herald, a woman with quicksilver eyes and movements so fluid she seemed to pass between shadows without touching the light between. She moved between worlds, witnessing the stark contrast between feast and famine. The Herald spoke of disturbing trends, how the Mills now produced twice the goods they had a decade ago, yet worker rations had been halved in the same time.

These whispers survived despite Laboria's elaborate propaganda system, designed to maintain the Spell of Necessity through constant reinforcement of the kingdom's natural order. Beginning in childhood, workers were immersed in carefully crafted narratives of their proper place and purpose.

The Town Criers represented the most visible arm of this system. Each morning, these officials in modest but immaculate uniforms positioned themselves at major intersections throughout the Gray Quarter. Their proclamations followed a calculated formula, one part praise for the Merchant King's wisdom, one part warning about the dangers of questioning established order, and one part announcement of reduced rations or increased quotas, always framed as opportunities for workers to demonstrate their dedication.

"Hear ye, hear ye!" called a Crier outside the Central Mill gates. "Praise be to His Prosperity the Merchant King, whose divine economics brings structure to our lives! Remember! Questioning production quotas brings chaos to the natural order! By royal decree, textile quotas increase by twenty percent effective immediately. His Prosperity offers this blessing so workers may demonstrate their gratitude through enhanced productivity!"

For children, indoctrination began in the Worker Preparation Centers, concrete buildings where young ones gathered while parents worked their shifts. There, instructors led daily recitations of the Laborer's Litany and conducted role-playing games where children practiced proper deference to authority.

"Who remembers the Three Virtues of Proper Workers?" asked an instructor, surveying a room of six-year-olds sitting on hard wooden benches.

"Gratitude, Diligence, Silence!" the children responded in practiced unison.

"Excellent! And what happens to ungrateful workers?"

"They cause suffering for everyone!" the children chanted, having memorized the response without understanding its implications.

The most sophisticated element of the propaganda system targeted adults through the Kingdom Knowledge Sessions, mandatory weekly meetings where supervisors delivered carefully crafted narratives. These sessions employed subtle psychological techniques, including group reinforcement of system-supporting statements and public shaming of any who showed insufficient enthusiasm.

"Let's remember together! Why do we work?" intoned a session leader to assembled textile workers.

"Because work gives meaning!" came the required response.

"And who provides our work?"

"His Prosperity the Merchant King!"

"And if the Merchant King did not organize our labor?"

"Chaos would reign! Starvation would follow! The kingdom would collapse!"

When one worker's response lacked sufficient conviction, the session leader paused dramatically. "Citizen Adler, perhaps you would benefit from additional Kingdom Knowledge reinforcement? The evening sessions include helpful memory aids."

Everyone understood these memory aids involved hours of standing in stress positions while reciting loyalty pledges. Citizen Adler immediately straightened her posture. "The kingdom would collapse, Session Leader! Without His Prosperity's guidance, we would surely perish!"

The leader nodded approvingly while making a note to monitor Citizen Adler in subsequent sessions.

Against this relentless machinery of manufactured consent, the Herald's whispers represented something revolutionary, factual information unfiltered by official narratives. When workers learned that the Merchant King had doubled his treasury while halving their rations, they were experiencing the first cracks in a lifetime of carefully constructed reality.

***

Throughout the Mill, whispered conversations sometimes touched on new ideas that challenged the Merchant King's narratives. Workers shared fragments of thoughts that, if pieced together, might form dangerous conclusions. These whispers never lasted long, a Guard's approaching footsteps or a supervisor's watchful eye would send them scattering like mice at a cat's shadow. But the seeds of questioning were being planted, even in minds like Eliza's that had long accepted the way of things.

She noticed changes in herself, small at first, then increasingly significant. Where once she had kept her eyes downcast when Guards passed, now she found herself watching them, studying their movements, identifying patterns in their patrols. Where she had once accepted reduced rations with resigned silence, she now found herself calculating exactly how much food had been taken and where it might have gone. These weren't yet revolutionary thoughts, but they were the first cracks in the foundation of acceptance that had structured her entire life.

As she worked her loom, fingers moving automatically through patterns practiced ten thousand times, her mind increasingly wandered to forbidden territory. Why did blankets that could save Gray Quarter lives warm Palace Heights beds? Why did fever lily medicine that could heal her daughter decorate noble dinner tables? The questions themselves felt dangerous, as if thinking them might somehow summon Guards to her doorstep.

Yet still she thought them, and with each passing day, the Spell of Necessity that had once seemed as immutable as the sunrise began to waver and thin, revealing glimpses of possibility beyond.

***

In the farthest corner of the Gray Quarter, in a tiny cottage distinguished only by its slightly more determined roof leak, Aldus Tanner, the Old Scholar, kept records and memories. His white hair and beard framed a face so deeply lined it resembled an ancient map, with wrinkles charting the territory of a lifetime's suffering and observation. Though his bones ached and his spectacles were held together with twine, his mind remained sharper than the Royal Council's decorative swords.

"It wasn't always like this," the Scholar would murmur to anyone who would listen, though few did. "Before the Mills, before the Merchant King's grandfather tripled the size of his counting house, people worked the land together. Harder in some ways, yes, but they kept what they grew."

The Scholar's eyes would then grow distant, clouded with memories that predated most Gray Quarter residents' births.

"I remember the last uprising," he told Eliza one evening, his voice dropping to a whisper though his cottage door was closed. The single candle between them cast long shadows across his lined face, deepening the history written there. "Thirty years ago, before your birth."

His hands trembled slightly as he pushed aside his meager dinner to make room on the table. With one gnarled finger, he traced patterns in the dust. Shapes slowly formed into buildings, figures, what appeared to be a Mill surrounded by tiny human forms.

"The Northern Mill workers organized what they called the 'Dignity Coalition.' Nothing radical. They asked for one additional rest day per month and the right to keep a fifth of their production rather than a tenth."

Eliza leaned closer, drawn by something in his voice, a tone usually reserved for speaking of the dead.

"The Merchant King's father sent in Guards from the Eastern Provinces. Not the regular ones you see in the streets. These wore black uniforms with no insignia. They sealed the Northern Mill with three hundred workers inside." He paused, his finger hovering over the dust-drawn Mill. "Then they introduced what they called 'The Cleansing Smoke' through the ventilation system."

"They killed them all?" Eliza asked, horror and disbelief warring in her voice.

The Scholar looked up, his glassy eyes suddenly sharp. "Worse. The smoke contained a substance that affected the mind. Removed inhibition. Induced rage." His finger smudged through the dust figures, disrupting their neat formation. "Worker turned against worker in a frenzy of violence."

He fell silent, lost in memory. Outside, a dog barked once and then quieted, as if aware it had said too much.

"The Guards watched through special windows," he finally continued. "Taking notes. Refining their technique."

"Why?" Eliza whispered.

"To learn the most efficient method of turning strength against itself. To discover how easily people become weapons against their own kind." His voice had gone flat, drained of emotion by years of carrying this knowledge.

"When they finally opened the doors three days later, only seventeen workers remained alive, covered in the blood of their neighbors. These survivors were paraded through every district, their minds shattered. Their purpose wasn't to warn us. It was to show us what we might become."

"Why doesn't anyone speak of this?"

The Scholar's laugh held no humor. "Those who witnessed it are dead or, like me, old enough to be dismissed as senile. The Guards who participated were eventually eliminated to remove evidence. The seventeen survivors died by their own hands within a year." His voice cracked. "My son was among those sealed in the Mill. My daughter-in-law was one of the seventeen. She never spoke again before walking into the river six months later."

"And your grandson?" Eliza asked, noticing for the first time a small wooden toy soldier half-hidden among the Scholar's few possessions.

The old man's expression closed like a door. "Became a Palace Guard. Believed the official story—that revolutionary agitators caused the violence. He despises me for spreading 'lies' about his parents' fate." His voice dropped to a whisper. "He now commands the special unit that handles 'labor unrest.' Commander Reeve, they call him. The cruelest of them all because he believes he's protecting the kingdom from chaos."

Eliza had heard that name before. Commander Reeve's tactics were legendary for their brutality, even among Palace Guards. The thought that the Scholar's blood ran in the veins of Laboria's most feared enforcer sent a chill through her.

"He was just a child when it happened," he said quietly. "Young enough to forget, old enough to be rewritten."

He wiped away the dust drawing with one hand. "Remember this, Eliza. The Merchant King's greatest weapon isn't the Guard, or hunger, or even fear. It is the distortion of memory. When people can't trust what they remember, they lose the ability to imagine anything different."

In Laboria, accurate memory was perhaps the most revolutionary act of all.

He looked at her again. The candlelight caught the pain in his eyes. "Beware the promise of perfect equity too. I've seen where it leads. The Eastern Realms once had a revolution that claimed to make everyone equal. They ended up with a hundred tyrants instead of one. Their fields withered. Their people starved. Misery was shared evenly. But it was still misery."

Few listened to warnings like his. The young rarely do, especially when the danger seems far away compared to the pain already at hand.

As she left his cottage that night, Eliza realized The Old Scholar had given her something dangerous, an unaltered piece of the past, a truth that contradicted official history. She carried it carefully, like something that might shatter if examined too closely or burn if held too tightly.

***

Nearby, in a tavern at the edge of the Gray Quarter, a different kind of voice had begun to draw attention. An Ambitious Orator, with eyes that burned like the Mills' furnaces, addressed the gathered workers in terms both poetic and fierce. His words were like kindling to a dangerous fire in the hearts of listeners.

"The prosperity dust does not rise naturally. It is stolen!" he declared. "The Magical Mills produce enough for all, yet we starve while they feast. The solution is simple. We must seize the Mills for ourselves, and then all will share equally in their bounty."

Ethan Forge, a master blacksmith known to most as the Pragmatic Craftsman, interrupted the monologue. His broad shoulders and hands bore the marks of thirty years shaping metal, his face weathered but thoughtful beneath iron-gray hair.

"But the Mills require specialized knowledge to operate," the Craftsman began. "Change may be needed, but total upheaval could bring collapse if no one understands the machinery."

"Silence, collaborator!" the Orator snapped, his momentary flash of anger quickly masked by a benevolent smile. "The Mills' 'complexity' is but another lie they tell us. Once we control them collectively, they will yield their secrets and their bounty to all."

The Craftsman fell silent, his weathered face showing not fear but patient concern, like a man watching storm clouds gather while others celebrated the changing weather. His hands, bearing the burns and scars of decades working with molten metal, would continue their steady work on whatever broken tool a neighbor had brought for repair.

"The complex machinery of the Mills requires careful maintenance and knowledge," the Craftsman confided to Eliza when they met at the communal well one dawn. The well's handle squeaked in protest as he drew water, the sound masked by the general morning bustle. "Revolutionary fervor cannot replace understanding of steam valves and pressure gauges."

"Then the revolution should preserve such knowledge, not discard it," Eliza replied, surprised by her own response. The word 'revolution', never before part of her vocabulary, had slipped from her lips as naturally as her own name.

The Craftsman studied her face. "Careful, Eliza Shaw. Such words have consequences. And revolutions rarely preserve what they claim to value."

***

That night, as Eliza kept vigil by Lily's bedside, she heard a tap at her window. Outside stood the Herald, face half-hidden by a hood.

"I have something," the Herald whispered, pressing a small vial into Eliza's hand. "Fever lily extract. Three drops every six hours."

Eliza stared at the vial, its contents glowing faintly in the moonlight, giving off a subtle scent of flowers and herbs. "I can't afford..."

"No payment," the Herald interrupted. "Consider it a gift from those who believe in a different future."

Before Eliza could ask more, the Herald was gone, melting into the shadows. With trembling hands, Eliza administered the medicine to Lily, watching as the child's breathing gradually eased.

By morning, Lily's fever had broken. As sunlight filtered through the patched curtains, casting weak patterns on the floor, Eliza made a silent vow. This system that valued ornamental flowers over children's lives, that produced magical blankets while allowing the poor to freeze, it could not stand. It would not stand.

Later that day, as workers trudged home from another exhausting day, Eliza paused outside the Magical Production Mills. She had spent fourteen hours crafting luxurious blankets embroidered with scenes of mythical feasts, yet her own child had nearly died in a bed covered with threadbare rags.

"Why," she wondered aloud, her voice gaining strength with each word, "do the Mills bring forth such bounty, yet our children know only hunger and sickness? Where does it all go?"

A passing Palace Guard heard her dangerous question and scowled. "Move along! Idle wondering leads to idle hands, and idle hands lead to the Royal Dungeons!"

Eliza met his eyes for the first time in her life, rather than looking at the ground as workers were trained to do. Something in her gaze, a new defiance, a refusal to be cowed, made the Guard step back.

He'd seen that look before, in men right before they threw themselves into machine gears to end it all. That look didn't blink. That look didn't beg. That look didn't fear.

"I said move along," he repeated, his voice less certain.

Eliza walked away, but the question had taken root in her mind like a seed that would not be dislodged. No longer was it just a question. It was a demand, a call to action.

And unbeknownst to her, the same transformation had begun in countless other minds throughout the Gray Quarter.

In that moment, though none yet realized it, the first tiny crack appeared in the Spell of Necessity, a crack that would soon widen into a chasm, releasing forces that would tear the kingdom apart.

That night, Eliza dreamed of her daughter playing in a meadow of fever lilies, the flowers abundant and free for all to use. It was a beautiful dream. But dreams born of hunger and suffering do not stay dreams for long.

ACT II

THE AWAKENING

A S WINTER'S GRIP TIGHTENED around the Gray Quarter, the thin blankets and thinner walls of workers' homes offered scant protection against the biting cold. Each morning, residents awoke to find frost patterns on the inside of their windows, beautiful crystalline formations that spelled out their vulnerability in nature's own handwriting.

In Eliza's cottage, Lily had recovered from her fever, but remained thin and pale. Her hair had lost some of its luster, and her cough echoed through their home like a grim reminder of what could have been and what still might be if their fortunes didn't change. Eliza had taken to wrapping her daughter in layers of clothing salvaged from discarded Mill scraps, creating a patchwork cocoon that rustled when Lily moved.

"I don't understand why we make these blankets for rich people but can't keep one for ourselves," Lily asked one evening as Eliza tucked her in, the child's breath visible in the frigid air.

Eliza's hands paused, her green eyes troubled. How could she explain to her ten-year-old that the very blankets her mother crafted were considered too valuable for the likes of them?

"The blankets need to travel far away," she answered finally. "To important people."

"We're not important?" Lily's innocent question hung between them, lingering like breath in the cold.

Eliza had seventeen different answers ready. She had rehearsed them during loom shifts and refined them while carrying water from the communal pump. All seventeen died in her throat.

Before she could formulate an answer that wouldn't plant seeds of either rebellion or worthlessness in her daughter's heart, a knock came at their door. Three quick taps, pause, two more. A pattern, not random. Few visitors called after curfew. It wasn't worth risking the Palace Guards' attention.

Opening the door a crack, Eliza found the Herald, face half-concealed beneath a hood crusted with ice crystals. Frost had formed in the woman's eyebrows, making them appear white, though she wasn't yet thirty.

"There's a meeting," the Herald whispered, her words emerging as little clouds that dissipated too slowly in the still air. "For those who ask questions."

Eliza glanced back at Lily. "I can't leave her alone."

"Bring her. There will be other children, and food." The Herald pressed something into Eliza's hand, a small red token with a symbol she didn't recognize. The metal felt oddly warm against her palm, as though it generated its own heat in defiance of winter's chill. "Show this at the old oak beyond the eastern well."

As the Herald turned to leave, she paused. "You won't be alone anymore, Eliza. That's what we offer. Not just ideas, but each other."

***

An hour later, wrapped in every layer they owned, Eliza and Lily made their way through streets emptied by cold and curfew. Palace Guards were scarce tonight. Even they preferred shelter to patrolling the frozen Gray Quarter. Still, Eliza's heart pounded whenever they passed the pools of light cast by street lanterns, feeling as exposed as a moth before the flame.

The old oak stood like a sentinel at the edge of the Quarter, its massive trunk split centuries ago by lightning yet somehow still alive, growing in two directions from the point of rupture. A fitting symbol, Eliza thought, for a kingdom divided against itself.

A figure materialized from behind the tree. "Your business?" a gruff voice demanded. He was a male, older, with a peculiar accent that suggested the eastern provinces.

Wordlessly, Eliza showed the red token. As it caught the moonlight, she noticed the symbol more clearly, a broken chain, the links separated but still recognizable.

The figure nodded and pointed to a narrow path leading into the forest. "Follow the red marks on the trees. You'll have to carry the little one if she tires."

The forest beyond the Kingdom's formal boundary had always been forbidden to Gray Quarter residents. "Wild beasts," the Palace Guards warned. "And dangerous out-laws." Yet as Eliza followed the path, marked by small red slashes on tree trunks, she felt a curious sense of liberation. Here, beyond Laboria's walls, the air itself seemed less con-strained.

It smelled different too. In the Gray Quarter, air was a stew of coal smoke, sewage, and the peculiar metallic tang of the Mills. Here, it carried traces of pine sap, decaying leaves, and something wilder that made her nostrils flare. Clean wasn't the right word. Undomesticated, perhaps. The scent of possibility.

After twenty minutes of walking, the trees opened into a clearing where a sight both wondrous and terrifying greet-ed them. At least a hundred people gathered around fire pits, talking in low, urgent voices. Most were workers from all Mills, identifiable by their clothing. And a few, most shocking of all, were wearing the regalia of Palace Heights servants.

The mood wasn't that of a desperate conspiracy but rather something closer to celebration. Small groups clustered around multiple fires, passing steaming mugs, sharing blan-kets against the cold. Somewhere, someone was playing a soft melody on a hand-carved flute, the notes dancing between the trees. Laughter, genuine laughter, not the bitter kind that echoed through Quarter taverns, rippled periodically through the gathering.

"Mama, look!" Lily tugged at her hand, pointing to something Eliza had missed in her assessment of the adults, a cluster of kids near one fire. They were being served bowls of steaming soup by an elderly woman with hands so gnarled they resembled tree roots.

Unlike the regimented children's activities in the Gray Quarter, designed primarily to prepare young bodies for Mill work, these children moved freely. A group played a game with carved wooden tokens, their laughter unrestrained. Others sat listening to an old man telling what appeared to be an actual story, not the dry recitations of the Merchant King's generosity that passed for education.

"Go," Eliza urged, giving her daughter a gentle push. "I'll be right over there." She watched as Lily approached the group hesitantly, then was welcomed with smiles and a generous bowl of soup that smelled better than anything they'd had in months. The scent reached Eliza even from a distance, real bone broth with herbs, not the thin gruel passed off as soup in the Gray Quarter.

A young girl with a tangled braid immediately made room for Lily, patting the log beside her. The seamlessness of this acceptance, no evaluations, no questions about family status or productivity ratings, struck Eliza. The child simply saw another child and moved to include her, a small act of compassion that seemed both ordinary and revolutionary.

As Eliza moved closer to the main gathering, a strange noise caught her attention, the sound of paper rustling. In the Gray Quarter, paper was precious, used primarily for official documents or, occasionally, letters to distant relatives penned by the few who could write. Yet here, dozens of people clutched pamphlets, reading them by firelight or listening as others read aloud.

A voice came from behind her. "First time?"

Eliza turned to find a woman about her age, with callused hands that marked her as a fellow textile worker. Unlike the downcast expressions that dominated the Mills, this woman's face was open, her eyes direct.

"Clara," the woman said. "Eastern Mill, loom section five."

"Eliza. Northern Mill, finishing department."

"Different Mills, same story." Clara's smile had a warmth that drew Eliza in immediately. "We've been neighbors in misery our whole lives without knowing it. But that ends now."

She led Eliza to a small fire where three other workers made space without hesitation. A man passed her a cup of something warm and fragrant, not tea exactly, but an herbal drink that seemed to chase the cold from her bones from the first sip.

"We were just discussing the Southern Mills' new policy," said a broad-shouldered man whom Clara introduced as Mikhail. "They're rotating shifts to prevent workers from forming connections."

"They do the same at Northern," Eliza offered, surprising herself with how easily she joined the conversation. "Every month, they scramble the teams."

"Exactly," Clara nodded. "Isolation is their most effective tool. That's why gathering like this terrifies them more than any weapon could."

Eliza realized she'd never before participated in a conversation among equals, where her observations were valued and her experience treated as expertise. The sensation was intoxicating, being heard, truly heard, perhaps for the first time in her life.

***

One particularly frosty morning a week earlier, a cart delivering Palace Heights' discarded newspapers to be recycled in the Mills had overturned on an icy cobblestone. Papers scattered across the square, and though most workers hurried past, Eliza had spotted a peculiar pamphlet that had landed at her feet. Unlike the gilded newspapers, this was crudely printed on rough paper.

Its title, stamped in bold red letters, read "The Book of Understanding: Why Workers Must Unite."

She had quickly tucked it into her shawl before the Guards noticed. That night, by the meager light of a tallow candle, she read words that seemed to articulate every frustration she had ever felt but never fully expressed.

The Book of Understanding wasn't printed on the fine parchment of Palace Heights documents or bound in leather like the volumes in the Merchant King's library. Its pages were rough, assembled from scraps of paper smuggled from Mill administrative offices, pressed flat and sewn together with textile worker's thread. The red ink of its title had been mixed from crushed berries and rust, giving it a dark, almost blood-like appearance that seemed fitting for its revolutionary content.

Running her fingers over the pages, Eliza felt a strange connection to its makers. The texture told a story of ingenuity and defiance. How many hands had worked in secret to produce this? How many small acts of courage had brought these words into existence? The paper itself seemed alive with shared purpose, rough edges and imperfect binding somehow more beautiful than any Palace Heights volume because it had been made with love rather than demanded through fear.

The pamphlet had passed through many hands before reaching Eliza's, each reader adding marginal notes, underlining passages that spoke most directly to their experience, occasionally adding personal testimonies of exploitation that echoed the text's arguments. These annotations created a sense of collective authorship, as if the Book had emerged organically from workers' shared suffering rather than from any single mind.

In one corner, a miner had sketched a small diagram of Palace Heights built atop a foundation of Gray Quarter workers. In another margin, a Mill worker had calculated exactly how many hours they worked compared to the value of goods produced, revealing a staggering disparity. These additions transformed what might have been abstract theory into visceral, lived reality.

As Eliza turned each page, she felt as though unseen walls in her mind were crumbling, walls built of explanations she'd been given since childhood about why some lived in luxury while others scraped by. The Book articulated a possibility she had scarcely permitted herself to imagine, that the entire system was deliberately designed to extract maximum labor for minimum compensation, that the "natural order" was in fact an artificial construct maintained through deliberate policy.

Most revolutionary of all was the Book's central argument, that workers didn't need the Merchant King or his administrators. They possessed all the skills required to run the Mills, distribute goods, and create a kingdom where prosperity flowed to all rather than concentrating at the top. This idea struck Eliza like a physical force. She had always assumed that the complex web of production and distribution required the expertise of Palace Heights officials. The notion that workers could manage it themselves, that they were the true source of all value, was both terrifying and exhilarating.

When she finally set the Book down, the tallow candle next to her burned to a stub, Eliza felt irrevocably changed. Where before she had seen only personal misfortune in Lily's illness and their poverty, she now recognized a systemic injustice. Where she had once felt isolated in her struggles, she now sensed potential allies in every fellow worker. Most dangerously of all, where she had once seen the Palace Guards as embodiments of unquestionable authority, she now perceived them as mere enforcers of an artificial and unjust arrangement.

She hid the Book beneath a loose floorboard, knowing possession of such material would mean severe punishment. But she couldn't hide the ideas it had planted. They took root in her mind, growing stronger with each new indignity she witnessed in the Mills, each new symptom of Lily's untreated illness, each new announcement of increased production quotas alongside decreased rations.

The most dangerous spell had been broken, not through magic, but through understanding.

***

The day after hiding The Book, Eliza arrived at her loom earlier than usual. Her mind raced with dangerous new thoughts, but her face remained carefully blank, a mask perfected through years of hiding pain, exhaustion, and hunger from Palace Guards who interpreted any sign of weakness as an excuse to reduce rations further.

Clara, who operated the loom beside Eliza's, noticed the change anyway. They had worked side by side for six years, developing the wordless communication of those who share confined spaces under constant surveillance.

"You look different," Clara whispered during a brief moment when the machinery's roar crescendoed, temporarily masking their voices. "Like you've seen something."

Eliza's hands maintained their steady rhythm at the loom, eyes forward. "Later," she murmured. "West water pump. After shift."

The water pump at the western edge of the Gray Quarter was one of the few gathering places where brief conversations didn't immediately attract Guard attention. Its constant squeaking masked quiet talk, and the necessity of water collection provided legitimate reason for workers to linger briefly.

As dusk fell, casting long shadows across the cobblestones, Eliza filled her bucket while Clara waited her turn.

"I found something," Eliza said, her voice barely audible above the pump's metallic complaints. "Words that explain everything."

Clara's eyes widened slightly, the most dramatic reaction safety permitted in public. "The Book? You've seen it too?"

The revelation that Clara already knew of the Book startled Eliza. She'd imagined herself one of very few who had encountered the forbidden text. "Who else?" she whispered.

"Viktor from the dye works. Marta from finishing. A few others." Clara pretended to check her bucket for leaks, buying seconds for conversation. "We meet sometimes. Talk about what it means."

"I want to join you," Eliza said, surprising herself with her own boldness.

Clara hesitated. "It's dangerous. Especially for someone with a child."

"It's more dangerous for Lily if nothing changes," Eliza replied, thinking of her daughter's fever, of medicines priced beyond reach.

After a moment's consideration, Clara nodded almost imperceptibly. "Third rest day. Bring scraps for patchwork. Come to my cottage. Just before curfew bells."

***

Clara's home was smaller than Eliza's, but somehow felt warmer. Perhaps it was the presence of five other workers, gathered in a tight circle around a single candle, their faces transformed by its flickering light from exhausted laborers to something more alive, more present. They called themselves The Understanding Circle. Not yet The Collective, just a handful of workers trying to make sense of ideas too dangerous to contemplate alone.

"We've each read pieces of The Book," explained Viktor, a thin man whose hands were permanently stained blue from the dye vats. "None of us has seen the entire text. That's safer. If one person is caught, they can't reveal what they don't know."

Eliza learned that similar circles had formed throughout the Gray Quarter, like raindrops gathering before becoming a stream. Each discussed particular passages from The Book, interpreted its meaning for their specific trades, and gradually connected to other circles through trusted intermediaries.

"The Merchant King's power depends on our isolation," whispered Marta, an older woman with deep lines etched around her eyes. "We've always seen our suffering as individual misfortune, not systematic exploitation."

These words, "systematic exploitation," struck Eliza like a physical blow. They named something she had felt but had lacked language to express.

For three hours they talked, sharing observations of Mill operations that suddenly made sense through The Book's lens. How production had doubled while rations decreased. How Palace Guards rotated frequently to prevent them developing sympathy for specific workers. How children were taught that their hunger was a personal failing rather than a deliberate policy.

What struck Eliza most was the quality of listening that pervaded the circle. Unlike the Mill foremen who interrupted workers mid-sentence or the Palace Guards who treated questions as insubordination, these people genuinely attended to each voice. When Henrik, usually reticent, spoke of his childhood in the Northern Provinces, everyone leaned in, valuing his perspective. When Marta expressed concerns about involving her grandchildren in revolutionary activities, no one dismissed her caution as cowardice but instead discussed ways to minimize risks for vulnerable families.

As the night progressed, the conversation shifted from analysis to practical considerations. Using materials at hand, Viktor demonstrated how Mill dyes could be repurposed to create inks for revolutionary messages. Clara showed how apparently innocent patterns woven into fabric could carry coded signals. Henrik explained how cutting room scraps, normally discarded, could be fashioned into surprisingly effective tools for disabling Mill machinery when necessary.

When the curfew bell rang, they departed individually, at staggered intervals. Eliza left with new words in her vocabulary and new awareness of how many shared her awakening.

***

Within weeks, Eliza could identify fellow awakened workers through nearly imperceptible signals, a particular way of folding one's work smock, a specific phrase woven into ordinary conversation, "The weather holds steady, though change approaches," a subtle gesture when passing in the street.

These codes emerged organically, adapting to increased Palace Guard vigilance. When authorities began monitoring gathering at water pumps, laundry lines became the new exchange point. When laundry areas fell under suspicion, children's games carried coded messages between households.

Most remarkable was how the language itself transformed. Words acquired new meanings, layered with revolutionary significance. "Understanding" meant far more than simple comprehension. "Necessary" became ironic, questioning what authorities deemed essential. "Collective" evolved from an abstract concept to an identity, whispered with growing pride.

Eliza watched her own behavior change in subtle ways. She made eye contact with fellow workers where before she would have looked down. She began to notice patterns in Palace Heights demands, how quotas always increased before noble celebrations, how rations always decreased when workers showed the slightest resistance.

Most telling was her reaction to Palace Guards. Where once she had felt helpless terror in their presence, she now experienced something more complex, outward deference masking inward defiance. This psychological shift, the ability to perform submission while maintaining private resistance, spread throughout the Gray Quarter, invisible to authorities but palpable among workers.

The first true test of their growing cohesion came unexpectedly. Jonas, who operated the steam valves at the Eastern Mill, collapsed from exhaustion during a sixteen-hour shift. The Mill Foreman ordered him taken to the Penalty Box, a small, unventilated chamber where workers were confined without food or water for productivity failures.

In the past, others would have looked away, grateful it wasn't them. This time, something different happened.

Berta, an elderly worker with little to lose, approached the Foreman. "Jonas needs water, not punishment," she said. Her voice trembled, but she stood her ground.

The Foreman sneered. "Back to your station, or join him."

Then Mikhail stepped forward. "She's right. He's sick, not lazy."

Then another worker. Then another.

Eliza, who had been halfway across the Mill floor, found herself moving toward the gathering without conscious decision. As she approached, Clara caught her eye from across the cluster of workers, a silent acknowledgment passing between them.

The Foreman's face reddened. "All of you to the Penalty Box, then!"

"There aren't enough boxes for all of us," someone called from the back.

It was a small moment. Not an outright rebellion, but a test of collective action. The workers didn't raise their voices or make threats. They simply stood, shoulder to shoulder, a living wall of quiet dignity.

The moment stretched, the only sound the relentless rhythm of machinery that continued its mechanical indifference to human concerns. Then something remarkable happened. The Foreman's eyes faltered. His gaze, usually fixed in unmovable authority, dropped momentarily to the floor.

"Fine," he muttered. "Give him water. Five minutes. Then back to work."

As workers dispersed, returning to stations before Guards could arrive, Eliza caught snippets of whispered exchanges.

> *"Did you see his face?"*
> *"He backed down!"*
> *"We did that."*

The victory was minuscule by any objective measure, one worker given brief relief, nothing more. Yet the impact rippled through the Mills like an invisible current. As Eliza returned to her loom, she noticed subtle changes all around her, straighter backs, higher chins, the faintest traces of smiles where none had existed before. They had discovered something powerful. Together, they could affect change.

***

These isolated moments of solidarity might have remained disconnected without the Herald, a woman who had once been a messenger between Mills before dismissal for harboring unproductive attitudes. Her knowledge of back routes and service tunnels made her invaluable for carrying news between Understanding Circles.

"You're not alone," she told each gathering. "The Western Mill workers have their own Circle. The Northern Textile workers are organizing. Even some Palace Heights servants are secretly sympathetic."

She brought more than information. She carried physical evidence of growing resistance. A red thread woven into work gloves from the Textile Mill. Bread rolls from the Palace kitchens, smuggled out by servants and distributed to the hungriest Gray Quarter children. Most precious of all, pages from The Book, passed between Circles to complete each group's understanding.

Through the Herald, Eliza learned about the Orator, a figure still shrouded in mystery but spoken of with growing reverence. "He understands both worlds," the Herald explained. "He can articulate our suffering in terms even Palace Heights can't dismiss."

Eliza was skeptical. "Why should we trust someone we haven't seen?"

The Herald's eyes gleamed. "You will see. He's calling together all Circles for a gathering. Not just whispers anymore, a true assembly of worker voices."

As the Herald turned to leave, Eliza caught her sleeve. "Why do you risk so much?" she asked, genuinely curious.

The woman's face softened. "When my sister died in childbirth because the midwife was busy attending a Palace Heights cat giving birth, I realized I had a choice. Die slowly from rage and grief, or channel it toward something meaningful." She glanced around to ensure they weren't observed, then continued, "Every message I carry, every Circle I connect, honors her memory. In this world, my sister was nothing. In the world we're building, she would have mattered."

The simple declaration resonated deeply with Eliza. It articulated something essential about the movement, that beyond abstract policies or distributional justice, they were fighting for human dignity, for the recognition that every life held inherent value.

***

What finally transformed these scattered Circles into a unified movement was, ironically, the Merchant King's own response to early signs of unrest.

When productivity first declined, Palace Guards increased random inspections. Workers were strip-searched leaving Mills, homes were entered without warning, and curfew violations were punished with public floggings rather than the usual fines. A loyalty bonus was announced, extra rations for workers who reported signs of collective thinking among their peers.

These measures, designed to crush nascent solidarity, instead accelerated it. Increased inspections meant workers developed more ingenious hiding places for forbidden materials. Intrusive searches created shared indignities that bonded even previously antagonistic workers. The loyalty program bred such distrust that workers realized their only security lay in deeper commitment to each other.

When Palace Guards burst into Eliza's cottage during dinner one evening, throwing open cupboards and upending her meager belongings in search of forbidden materials, Lily's eyes had widened in fear. But something unexpected happened once they left. Neighbors appeared at her door, one by one, bringing small offerings, a mended blanket to replace one the Guards had torn, a few precious matches to relight her fire, a cup of watery soup for Lily.

"They came to my place yesterday," whispered Viktor, handing her a tiny jar of ointment for her scraped knuckles. "They'll go to someone else tomorrow. But we'll always help each other afterward. That's how we win."

This spontaneous mutual aid, this instinctive community response to oppression, moved Eliza deeply. In the Mills, workers had been conditioned to see each other as competitors for limited resources. Now, that artificial division was dissolving in the face of shared hardship.

Most consequential was the public punishment of Silas, an elderly machinist accused of sabotage after a loom broke under his care. Everyone knew the machinery had failed from overuse and poor maintenance, but the Merchant King demanded an example.

The Guards dragged Silas to the central square, forcing the entire Gray Quarter to witness his punishment, twenty lashes before his trembling family. The deliberate cruelty, meant to instill terror, instead crystallized simmering resentment into cold resolve.

That night, red marks appeared throughout the Quarter, small, stylized broken chains chalked on walls, etched into work benches, woven subtly into repair patches on clothing. No one took credit, yet by morning they were everywhere, visible symbols of what had previously been invisible connection.

When Guards scrubbed the symbols away, twice as many appeared the next night. When they posted watchmen, the marks appeared behind them, as if materialized from thin air. It became something of a game, workers competing to place symbols in ever more audacious locations. Once, they even did it on the back of a Guard's uniform, unrealized until he returned to Palace Heights to jeers from his compatriots.

Each new symbol represented more than mere defiance. It was a message to fellow workers, you are not alone. The broken chains appearing overnight told a story without words. What seems permanent can be broken, what appears unbreakable is already fracturing.

***

Before he became the voice of revolution, Alaric Welles had seen both worlds.

Born the son of a Palace Heights minor official, he had occupied that rare space between kingdoms, not nobility, but adjacent enough to catch their scent. His father, a thin man who never stopped straightening the buttons on his uniform, inspected Mill operations with a clipboard and tight smile. Young Alaric would accompany him, walking between the looms, watching while trying to be invisible.

He was twelve the first time he truly saw.

A girl, perhaps seven, collapsed at her station, fingers bleeding into the fine blue silk destined for Palace Heights tables. The foreman nudged her with his boot, not unkindly, just tired. "Up, little bird. Quota's not met." When she didn't move, he signaled to an older woman who collected the small body without expression, carrying her to a side room where other exhausted children waited to recover. Or not.

Alaric looked at his father, expecting outrage or intervention. His father was writing on his clipboard, mouth pursed in concentration. "Wasteful inefficiency," he muttered. "Recovery procedures require streamlining."

That night, watching his father pick at dessert, crystallized berries arranged in the pattern of the royal crest, Alaric asked, "Why did you do nothing about the girl?"

His father's spoon paused halfway to his mouth. "What girl?"

"The one who collapsed. At the Mill."

Something closed in his father's face. It wasn't cruelty, but the careful blankness that comes from practiced justification. "That's how things work, Alaric. Natural order. Some lead, others follow. Some feast, others hunger. It has always been so."

"But it's not natural," Alaric said, the words unfurling something dangerous inside him. "It's built. Designed. Maintained."

His father studied him for a long moment before sighing. "You'll understand when you're older. There's a necessary distance between knowing how things work and questioning why they must work that way."

The breaking point came four years later.

His father took him to witness the Merchant King's response to a work slowdown in the Eastern Mill. Workers and their families were gathered outside while those inside were denied food and water for three days. Alaric watched a mother press herself against the locked gate, calling her child's name until her voice gave out. Palace Guards stood impassively, wearing the practiced detachment his father had perfected.

When several children died of dehydration, the Merchant King declared it a regrettable but instructive outcome.

That night, Alaric couldn't sleep. He crept into his father's study, searching for understanding or justification. He found neither. Instead, he discovered truth in ledgers and reports. Productivity tripled while worker compensation halved. Recommendations for reduced rations to increase "compliance motivation." Studies on minimum caloric intake required to maintain productivity without "premature worker depletion."

Most damning was a memorandum in his father's handwriting. "The ideal worker experiences enough hunger to ensure compliance but insufficient hunger to permit expiration before replacement training costs are recouped."

People calculated like resources. Lives measured against cost. Children's deaths as instructive outcomes.

Alaric took the documents and left that night, slipping past the drowsy gate guard with the ease of someone who belonged. He did not go quietly into revolutionary fervor. His transformation took years of living among workers, of experiencing the conditions he had previously only observed, of learning to hunger not just in philosophy but in body.

The documents became the factual foundation of what would evolve into The Book of Understanding. But something else formed in him too, something no document captured. The realization that his father's methodical cruelty might be necessary to fight his father's methodical cruelty. That achieving justice might require the same cold calculation that had created injustice.

He never spoke of his origins to his followers. Better they believe he had risen organically from their ranks, a pure expression of worker consciousness. Better they never glimpse the part of him that remained his father's son, the part that understood exactly how to manage human resources for maximum output, whether that output was silk or revolution.

Now, almost twenty years later, Alaric had become the Orator, his voice igniting the very revolution whose seeds had been planted that day in the Mill when he witnessed a child collapse over fabric destined for tables he once ate upon.

***

The cellar smelled of damp earth and something metallic, like old coins forgotten in a pocket, or blood. Eliza followed the Herald down uneven stone steps, guided by the faint glow of red-tinted lamps. The space had once stored winter vegetables. Now it stored something more volatile, revolutionary commitment.

They called it The Crucible, this underground room where The Collective tested the metal of its members. Eliza had thought her attendance at meetings, her distribution of pamphlets, her small acts of Mills resistance had proven her loyalty. She was wrong.

Twelve figures waited, seated in a semicircle, faces shadowed beneath hoods despite the privacy the cellar already provided. At the center stood the Orator, his eyes catching the red light like embers.

"Comrade Eliza," he began, his voice both welcoming and evaluative, "loyalty to our cause requires more than intellectual agreement. Ideas alone are bloodless. Belief must be demonstrated through action."

A bundle was placed on the stone floor before her. The Orator unwrapped it slowly, revealing a Palace Guard's uniform, its fabric still holding the shape of its previous owner. The cloth retained a faint scent of sweat and the pine-tar soap issued to Guards, and something else beneath. Something copper-bright and raw.

"This belonged to Supervisor Trent of the Northern Mill," he explained. The name sent ice through Eliza's veins. Trent's reputation among female workers was spoken of only in whispers, the special inspections that left young women hollow-eyed, the "reassignments" that followed complaints against him.

"Three days ago, revolutionary justice found him," the Orator continued, producing a knife from within his robe. Its blade caught the red light, transforming it into something liquid.

The test was clear. Eliza was to desecrate the uniform, to strike symbolically at what Trent represented. But as she reached for the knife, a hooded figure spoke from the shadows.

"Not enough," said a woman's voice, familiar somehow, though Eliza couldn't place it. "Revolutionary commitment requires personal risk. Comrade Eliza must wear a piece of this uniform to her next shift."

The air in the cellar changed, charged with new danger. This was no longer symbolic. Discovery meant imprisonment, possibly worse. Eliza's fingers closed around the knife's handle, cool against her palm. She thought of Lily waiting at home, of the precarious safety she'd created for them both.

Then she thought of the girls Trent had cornered in storage rooms, of trembling hands threading looms afterward, of eyes that never quite focused again. She remembered one young woman in particular. Mira, barely sixteen, who had thrown herself into the millrace after a special inspection in Trent's office. The body had floated past the loading docks at shift change, ensuring maximum visibility, a final protest the girl never lived to see.

With deliberate movements, Eliza sliced the Palace crest from the uniform's sleeve. The fabric resisted, then yielded with a sound like a final exhale. Using a needle and thread from her pocket, a weaver is never without her tools, she sewed the emblem inside her own work smock, positioning it over her heart, hidden but present.

"I will wear the enemy's mark in secret," she declared, meeting the Orator's gaze steadily, "as he wore the mask of authority while practicing violation."

Something shifted in the Orator's expression, approval tinged with something else. Reassessment, perhaps. The hooded figures murmured their acceptance. The test was passed.

Only later, lying awake beside sleeping Lily, did Eliza fully comprehend what had happened in that cellar. The test wasn't merely to assess her hatred of the enemy or her willingness to take risks. It revealed something more fundamental about the revolution itself, that intellectual agreement was insufficient, that physical demonstration of commitment was required, that those who hesitated deserved suspicion.

The contradiction troubled her. The revolution promised liberation from the Merchant King's arbitrary demands, yet imposed its own tests of worthiness. It claimed to value each worker equally, yet clearly separated true believers from mere sympathizers.

She touched the hidden emblem sewn against her skin. The threads itched. The patch's weight felt heavier than it should, like a stone rather than fabric.

In fighting monsters, how careful must one be not to adopt their methods? The question formed and then dissolved as exhaustion claimed her, the Guard's crest a hard secret pressed against her heart.

***

The abandoned flour mill on the Quarter's western edge had been repurposed as The Collective's People's Assembly Hall. Its grinding stones long silent, the space now served a different purpose, organizing worker resistance and building alternative community structures.

Eliza attended meetings there twice weekly, finding the atmosphere electric with purpose. Workers who had spent lifetimes bent in submission now stood straight, voicing ideas and sharing skills. The space itself had been transformed through collective effort, cleaned, repaired, and decorated with revolutionary symbols. Benches crafted from discarded lumber provided seating arranged in concentric circles to facilitate discussion.

Most revolutionary of all was the children's area, where Lily and others engaged in actual education rather than the rote memorization of Palace Heights propaganda that passed for schooling in the Quarter. Here, children learned reading and mathematics alongside revolutionary principles, developing both practical skills and political consciousness.

Eliza found herself joining the textile committee, where her experience with the Mills' most complex looms made her expertise valuable. For the first time, her knowledge was acknowledged and respected rather than extracted without recognition. The committee had ambitious goals, creating alternative production methods that could eventually supply the Quarter's needs without Palace Mills, developing fabrics durable enough to withstand Gray Quarter conditions yet affordable for worker families.

"Imagine clothing designed for actual humans instead of Palace decoration," said Marta, the committee's coordinator, during one particularly inspiring session. "Garments that keep children warm in winter rather than showcasing nobles' wealth. Fabrics that stand up to real work instead of dissolving at the first hint of effort."

The revolutionary framework transformed not just how they worked but what they created. Designs emerged based on worker needs rather than Palace desires, simple, durable garments with hidden pockets for carrying revolutionary materials, reinforced seams that wouldn't split during hard labor, cloth treatments that resisted the Quarter's perpetual damp. Each innovation represented not just technical improvement but political statement, that worker comfort mattered, that their bodies deserved protection, that their needs warranted consideration.

Lily thrived in the revolutionary children's program, returning home with new knowledge and growing confidence. She learned to read with surprising speed, devouring any text she could find with the enthusiasm of someone discovering a new sense. Her natural intelligence, which Palace education would have systematically suppressed, blossomed under revolutionary teaching that valued critical thinking alongside practical skills.

Through collective organization, Quarter residents had begun addressing problems Palace Heights had neglected for generations. A rotating maintenance team repaired communal water pumps promptly when they failed. A shared childcare system allowed parents working opposite shifts to ensure their children were never left alone. Food redistribution networks ensured that surpluses reached those in greatest need rather than being hoarded or wasted.

"It's all about solidarity in practice, not just theory," Clara explained while helping organize a communal cooking space where workers could prepare meals together, sharing limited fuel and ingredients to create more nourishing food than individual cooking allowed. "We're not just talking about a better world, we're building it right now, with whatever we have."

This practical dimension of revolution, the immediate improvements to daily life, convinced many who might have remained skeptical of abstract ideology. The community building wasn't just preparation for some future victory, but tangible benefits in the present. Collective action had already reduced the number of children dying from preventable illness, improved sanitation in the most neglected areas, and created information networks that warned of Guard raids and dangerous Mill conditions.

After one assembly meeting, Eliza found herself walking alongside the Pragmatic Craftsman as they left the hall. The night was unusually clear, stars visible through gaps in the Quarter's perpetual haze. The blacksmith's large frame cast a long shadow in the moonlight as they navigated the uneven cobblestones.

"Your textile designs are impressive," he said after they had walked in companionable silence. "Practical solutions for real problems. That's the kind of revolutionary work I believe in."

"You don't sound convinced about other aspects," Eliza ventured, noting the careful way he had emphasized 'that kind.'

The Craftsman glanced around before responding, his voice lowered. "The revolution offers hope, but hope isn't enough. Building requires more than tearing down." He gestured toward a water pump they were passing, recently repaired by the maintenance collective. "That pump works because someone understood its mechanism, not because they believed passionately in water access."

"You believe we need both," Eliza said. "Passion and practical knowledge."

"I believe a revolution that discards expertise in favor of ideology will eventually leave people thirstier than before." The moonlight caught in his iron-gray hair as he nodded toward her cottage. "But I'll keep making tools for the future, whatever shape it takes. Perhaps you'll keep making cloth that actually serves those who need it."

With that, he tipped his cap and continued on his way, his steady footsteps fading into the night sounds of the

Quarter. His words remained with Eliza as she entered her home, finding Lily already asleep, a revolutionary pamphlet still clutched in her small hand. For all the meetings and manifestos, it was the tangible improvements that mattered most to their daily lives.

In her more reflective moments, Eliza recognized that the revolution was offering something beyond material improvements or political transformation. It provided meaning, a framework for understanding suffering not as random misfortune but as systematic injustice that could be collectively addressed. It offered agency, the possibility of changing conditions rather than merely enduring them. Perhaps most importantly, it created community, genuine bonds between people previously isolated by Palace Heights' deliberate atomization strategies.

***

In Palace Heights, the first hints of trouble had begun to penetrate the Merchant King's consciousness. Production quotas were not being met. More workers called in sick than ever before. Strange symbols appeared on delivered goods, sometimes visible, sometimes hidden beneath linings or inside seams where only the recipient would find them.

"A minor nuisance, Your Prosperity," assured Lord Puffinbottom at an emergency meeting of the Royal Council. His jowls quivered as he spoke, tiny droplets of spittle flying from his lips. He'd grown fatter since winter began, while Gray Quarter children grew thinner. "The Gray Quarter occasionally experiences these spasms of ingratitude. They will pass once their bellies grow empty enough."

Lady Silkenpurse nodded, the jewels in her elaborate headdress catching the light like predatory eyes. "Perhaps a further reduction in rations would remind them of their dependence on your benevolence?"

The Merchant King stroked his jeweled beard. Each stroke made a soft clicking sound as rings collided with the metal and gemstone threads woven into the facial hair. "Double the Palace Guard presence around the Mills. Any worker heard speaking of 'collective' anything is to be reported immediately."

Only one councilor, a duchess who had once been a Mill overseer before marrying into nobility, seemed concerned. Her hands, though now softened by luxury, still showed faint scars from her years among the machinery. "The discontent appears more organized than previous incidents. There are rumors of a book circulating."

"Absurd!" huffed Lord Puffinbottom. His face had turned the same shade as his ruby-colored waistcoat. "Three-quarters of the Gray Quarter can barely read their own names, let alone revolutionary texts. Besides, books don't feed hungry mouths."

The Merchant King raised a hand for silence. "Nevertheless, increase the reward for informants. I want to know who is behind this irritation."

News of the increased Guard presence and informant rewards reached The Collective through the Herald, whose cousin served as a laundress in Palace Heights. Rather than dampening revolutionary fervor, the news energized it. The

Merchant King's concern confirmed what The Book of Understanding had claimed, that worker solidarity represented genuine power that could shake even Palace Heights' confidence.

"They fear us," the Orator announced at an emergency gathering. "Not our individual actions, which they could easily crush, but our unified resistance, which they cannot."

His words rippled through The Collective, strengthening resolve rather than instilling fear. Guards could arrest individuals, but they couldn't imprison a movement that had taken root in thousands of minds. Informants might identify some revolutionaries, but they couldn't betray an idea that had already spread beyond containment.

***

On the night of the forest gathering, as Eliza and Lily made their way through the darkness, they were no longer isolated individuals defying authority, but part of something larger, a movement that had grown organically from shared suffering into shared purpose.

The Understanding Circles, once scattered and secretive, had gradually connected through an intricate web of trusted relationships. The coded languages had evolved into explicit revolutionary vocabulary. The subtle symbols had become open declarations of allegiance. The hesitant solidarity had hardened into collective identity.

This transformation hadn't happened overnight. It had developed through thousands of small interactions, shared glances, whispered conversations, minor acts of mutual support, and cautious tests of collective power. Each step too small to trigger decisive repression, together they created something Palace Heights hadn't anticipated and couldn't easily destroy.

As they approached the gathering place, Eliza realized how much had changed in just a few months. The Book had awakened understanding, yes, but it was the lived experience of gradual unification that had truly broken the Spell of Necessity.

The forbidden question, "Why must things be this way?" had become "How can we make things different?"

And now, as workers gathered from all Quarters to hear the Orator, it was transforming into a declaration. "Things WILL be different."

What none yet realized, not even Eliza with her growing doubts, was that the very processes which had liberated their minds from one spell were forging the chains for another. The secret languages, the us-versus-them thinking, the elevation of solidarity above all other values, the growing intolerance for dissent within their ranks, these were not just tools of liberation but seeds of a new kind of conformity.

But on that night, as hundreds of workers assembled in defiance of curfew and custom, such concerns seemed remote. The revolution felt like pure possibility, a collective awakening to shared power. The Orator was about to speak, and with him, a new vision of Laboria would emerge, one that promised to shatter the old hierarchies forever.

Or so they believed.

"Workers of Laboria!"

The voice sliced through the clearing's murmurs, not by volume but by something in its quality, a resonance that bypassed the ear and vibrated directly in the chest.

The Orator had begun to speak.

"The chains that bind you are not forged of iron but of ideas. Your labor creates all wealth, yet you starve while others feast on the fruits of your toil. The Magical Mills run on nothing more magical than your sweat and skill, yet you are told the prosperity they create must flow upward by natural law. This is the greatest deception in history!"

Unlike the bombastic proclamations of Palace Heights officials, his voice was measured, intimate, as if sharing secrets with close friends rather than addressing a crowd. He spoke in bursts and pauses that created a rhythm almost like the Mills' machinery, a pulse that workers felt in their bones, familiar yet transformed.

"Friends, comrades," he continued, the firelight catching the hollows of his cheeks, his eyes reflecting the flames until they seemed to burn from within, "you have each found your way here because you have begun to see through the Spell of Necessity. You have asked the forbidden question. Why must we, who create everything, own nothing?"

Murmurs of agreement rippled through the crowd.

"The Book of Understanding reveals what the Merchant King and his lackeys have hidden for generations. There is no magic in the Mills except the magic of human labor! We built them, we operate them, and yet we are told we must be grateful for the crumbs that fall from Palace Heights' tables."

As he spoke, Eliza noticed how the tensions seemed to leave people's bodies. Backs straightened. Eyes lifted. It was as if invisible weights were being removed, burdens of shame and resignation set down after being carried for generations.

The Orator continued, his voice rising with controlled passion. "Just yesterday, in the Western Quarter, three more children died. Not from some mysterious ailment, not from bad luck or cruel fate, but from hunger. Deliberate, manufactured hunger in a kingdom where Palace Heights kitchens throw away more food each evening than would feed those children for a year!"

A woman near Eliza began to weep quietly, and Eliza realized with a jolt that she must be from the Western Quarter, perhaps even a relative of those lost children. The woman's hands were stained indigo from the dye works, her nails permanently blue-black despite scrubbing. She twisted a small cloth doll in her fingers as she wept, perhaps the only possession she'd been able to save from her child's belongings.

Without thinking, Eliza reached out and took the woman's hand. The stranger's fingers clutched hers with desperate strength, calloused skin against calloused skin, a connection between two mothers who understood loss without needing explanations. This too felt revolutionary, to comfort a stranger, to acknowledge grief publicly, to share the burden of emotion that Quarter life had taught them to hide.

"I have seen a vision of another world," the Orator proclaimed, his eyes gleaming with fervor. "A world where the

Mills belong to those who work them, where prosperity is shared by all, where no child goes hungry while another gorges on seventeen-course feasts!"

The crowd's response grew more enthusiastic with each proclamation. Eliza felt herself swept up in the collective emotion, a sense of possibility that had never before seemed within reach.

Only one voice cut against the tide of approval. The Pragmatic Craftsman stepped forward, his weathered face illuminated by the firelight.

"I share your anger at the injustice we face," he said cautiously, his thick fingers absently tracing woodgrain patterns on his palm, a craftsman's habit. "But I've maintained the inner workings of the Mills for twenty-three years. Their operation requires..."

"Technical details that concern only those who wish to maintain the current system!" interrupted the Orator, with a dismissive wave. "Once liberated from exploitation, we will solve these matters collectively."

"But the distribution networks, the maintenance requirements, the specialized knowledge," persisted the Craftsman, his voice gaining the sharp edge of someone who has spent decades being ignored by those who should listen.

A chorus of voices drowned out the Craftsman. "Collaborator!" someone shouted from the darkness. "He speaks the language of Palace Heights!"

The Orator raised his hands for silence. "Our friend is simply conditioned by years of being told only a select few can understand the Mills' mysteries. This is precisely the lie we must reject! The Book of Understanding teaches us that workers' collective wisdom exceeds any individual expert's knowledge."

The Craftsman fell silent, though his expression remained troubled. Something flashed in his eyes. Not fear, exactly, but a weary recognition, as though watching a scene he'd witnessed before with a different cast. Eliza felt a momentary unease, his concerns seemed practical rather than ideological, but the sensation was quickly submerged beneath the intoxicating current of revolutionary fervor.

As the meeting continued, Eliza made her way to the children's circle, where Lily sat listening wide-eyed to a story told by a gray-haired woman. Not a fairy tale of the sort Palace Heights children might hear, but a story of the time before, when land was worked communally, when harvests were shared equally, when no palace loomed above ordinary homes.

"Is that true?" Lily whispered to Eliza when she sat down beside her. "Was there really a time when everyone had enough?"

Eliza hesitated. She didn't know if the story was historical fact or revolutionary mythology. And in that moment, she wasn't sure it mattered.

"There could be such a time again," she answered, surprising herself with her conviction.

That night, a dozen children gathered near one fire began to sing. The melody was simple but haunting, combining traditional Quarter folk tunes with new revolutionary lyrics. Their voices, high and clear in the night air, carried a poignant mix of hope and determination.

"Where once we hungered in silence,
Now together we rise and stand.
The chains that bound our parents,
Are broken in our hands.

The Mills that ground our bodies,
Will serve all equally.
The future dawns for children,
In a land where all are free."

Many adults wiped away tears as the children sang. The revolution's ultimate purpose, creating a better world for the next generation, had never been more clearly expressed than in these young voices singing of a future they had never experienced but could now imagine.

As dawn broke, bringing another day of revolutionary activities, Eliza pushed her lingering doubts away. Such thinking was dangerous, not because it was wrong, but because it threatened both the old order and the new one taking shape.

She rose and prepared for the day, pinning her revolutionary emblem to her shawl with fingers that no longer hesitated. Outside, the Gray Quarter stirred with new energy, the collective awakening that would soon transform into rebellion.

The revolution that had begun in whispers would soon speak with the full voice of the people. For better or worse, the Quarter would never be the same. As Eliza stepped into the weak morning light, she believed with all her heart that whatever came next would be better than what they were leaving behind. The future beckoned, red as the dawn breaking over Laboria's uneven rooftops.

"Are you ready, Lily?" she called, helping her daughter button her worn coat.

"Ready, Mama," the girl replied, her revolutionary badge gleaming against the faded fabric. "We're making history, aren't we?"

"Yes," Eliza said, taking her daughter's hand as they stepped into the street together. "We're making history instead of just suffering it."

Nearly six months had passed since she first discovered The Book of Understanding, half a year of slow awakening and growing resistance. In that time, the Quarter had changed more than in the previous decade. People who once avoided each other's eyes now exchanged secret greetings. Neighbors who once competed for scarce resources now shared them freely. Children who had been taught only obedience now learned to question and create.

And in that moment, as she walked with Lily toward another day of building this new world, Eliza's doubts seemed as insubstantial as morning mist burning away in the rising sun. The concerns the Craftsman had raised about expertise, the warnings Aldus had shared about past rebellions, even her own unease about the tests of loyalty, all receded before the warmth of hope, fragile but real, that they were creating something genuinely better.

The path ahead might not be perfectly clear, but it led forward, away from certain misery and toward possible joy. There would be struggles, perhaps even dangers, but they would face them together, bound by something stronger than the chains that had held them before.

As mother and daughter rounded the corner toward the Assembly Hall, the morning sun caught the broken chain emblem on Eliza's shawl, transforming the crude red symbol into something almost luminous. For now, that light was enough to guide their way.

Act III

THE HOLLOW VICTORY

S PRING ARRIVED IN LABORIA, slipping through the kingdom like a thief taking the cold but leaving little comfort in its wake. In the Gray Quarter, the new season brought no relief. The Merchant King, alarmed by reports of unrest, had decreased rations further to encourage productivity and doubled the Palace Guard's presence around the Mills. Workers now entered their shifts through corridors of armored men, each face scrutinized for signs of rebellious intent.

The Guards had developed a new technique. They would stand perfectly still, then suddenly shift position when a worker passed. It startled the nerves and made people flinch. Those who flinched too violently were pulled aside for loyalty verification. Most didn't return to the shift line. Fewer returned to their homes.

For Eliza, the new season meant watching Lily grow thinner despite the seasonal abundance that should have followed winter's scarcity. At twelve years old, Lily was still too thin, but she no longer had the ghostly frailty of younger children in the Gray Quarter. Her collarbones remained sharp beneath her skin, but her posture had straightened, and a wiry strength had begun to take hold. Dark circles shadowed her eyes, giving her the appearance of someone far older, a miniature adult trapped in a child's failing body. Yet when Eliza suggested skipping a Collective meeting to rest, Lily protested with surprising vehemence.

"I'm a Young Pioneer of the Revolution," she insisted, her small face pinched with determination. Her left foot tapped a rhythm against the floor, tap-tap-pause-tap, a new habit that emerged whenever she recited revolutionary phrases. "We're making cards to identify class enemies."

The words sent a chill through Eliza that had nothing to do with the spring rain seeping through their cottage roof. That roof had developed seven distinct leaks, each with its own personality. The one above the door dripped in perfect rhythm, like a timekeeper. The one near the hearth made no sound at all. Water simply appeared in expanding circles on the floor, as if materializing from nowhere. The worst was the one above Lily's bed. It was irregular and unpredictable, sometimes stopping for days before releasing a sudden cascade precisely when they'd convinced themselves it had healed.

Lily had begun bringing home drawings from the children's meetings, crude sketches of Palace Guards and nobles being punished for their crimes. The figures were rendered with the odd proportions of new artists, awkward limbs and oversized heads, but the violence depicted was disturbingly specific and anatomically accurate. Guards with eyes gouged out. Nobles hanging from makeshift gallows, tongues protruding at precise angles. Merchant families drowning in pools of their own blood.

Sometimes the sketches depicted ordinary Gray Quarter residents too, labeled with red Xs and phrases like hoarder or thought-criminal that a child Lily's age shouldn't know, let alone use with such casual certainty. The phrases were always written in perfect cursive, clearly added by adult hands guiding the children's educational art.

***

The first true rebellion began not with a grand proclamation or violent uprising, but with a simple absence.

One Monday morning, the weaving section of the Eastern Mill stood silent. Fifty workers had failed to appear for their shift. Not one or two, which happened often enough when sickness or Guard brutality claimed lives, but fifty at once. The machines, accustomed to constant motion, seemed to hold their breath in the unnatural stillness.

The silence itself felt subversive.

Palace Guards were dispatched to their homes, only to find each door bearing a small red mark and the occupants nowhere to be found. The marks varied slightly, some perfect circles, others with tiny rays extending outward like suns. To untrained eyes, they might have passed for ordinary damage or children's play. To the Guards, trained in detecting patterns, they signaled coordination, intent, defiance.

Eliza was among the absent. The previous night, she and Lily had joined other weavers and their families at a predetermined gathering point, where they were led through a series of underground tunnels, remnants of an ancient mining system, to the forest beyond Laboria's borders. The children had treated it as an adventure, but the adults understood the gravity of their action. They had crossed from protest to open rebellion. There would be no return to normal life, no possibility of claiming ignorance or coercion if captured.

The exodus had been meticulously planned over months. Small groups of workers were instructed to leave their homes at staggered intervals, following different routes to avoid drawing attention. Eliza and Lily had departed under cover of darkness, carrying only what they could fit in two small bundles, warm clothes, Eliza's sewing tools, and the fever lily medicine that had become increasingly scarce in the Gray Quarter. Eliza had also tucked away something forbidden, Thomas's last letter, the paper so worn from repeated folding and unfolding that the creases had become translucent.

When they reached the old grain storehouse that served as the gathering point, they found it transformed. The rotting floorboards had been removed to reveal a narrow staircase descending into darkness. A young man wearing the red armband of The Collective's Security Committee checked their names against a list before permitting them to enter. His eyes never blinked during the entire exchange. This was a trait common to those who worked security, as though they feared missing something crucial in that split second of darkness.

"Comrades," he whispered, his voice carrying the peculiar hoarse quality of someone accustomed to speaking this way, "remember the three rules of underground passage, absolute silence, stay close to the person ahead, and obey guide signals without question."

Lily clutched her mother's hand as they descended the stairs, her small face both frightened and exhilarated. She had never been underground before. The darkness had texture here, thick enough to touch, with a mineral taste that coated the tongue. At the bottom, they joined a group of fifteen workers and their families. The Herald stood at the front, holding a shielded lantern that cast just enough light to illuminate the immediate path ahead. The lantern's glow reflected oddly in her eyes, making them appear amber rather than their usual brown.

"We follow the old mining tunnels," she explained in hushed tones. "They were sealed during the Great Collapse fifty years ago, but The Collective has been secretly restoring passages for months. Palace Heights doesn't know they exist. Their maps were deliberately falsified after the collapse to prevent worker escapes."

The tunnels were cramped and damp, requiring adults to stoop and children to be carried through certain sections. Eliza's back developed a peculiar ache, not just from bending but from the constant tension of anticipating the moment when the ceiling would lower further still. The air grew thick and stale as they progressed deeper, occasionally opening into larger chambers where mining equipment lay abandoned, frozen in time. In one such chamber, rusted carts still held ore that would never reach the surface, their contents now transformed into strange crystalline formations that glimmered in the lantern light. The crystals grew in spiral patterns, resembling tiny frozen whirlpools caught in mid-rotation.

Eliza noticed markings on the walls, faded carvings left by miners generations ago. Some were practical indicators of depth or direction, but others depicted scenes of worker solidarity. They showed stylized figures standing together, hands linked against unseen forces. Some showed workers battling creatures with too many limbs and fanged mouths, metaphors for mine collapses, perhaps, or for the more mundane horrors of exploitation. The Pragmatic Craftsman, walking nearby, noticed her interest.

"The miners were the first to organize," he whispered, his breath warm against her ear. "Long before The Book of Understanding reached Laboria. Their collective resistance was crushed so completely that Palace Heights erased it from official history. But they left these messages for future workers."

His words reminded Eliza of their first meeting at the communal well, when he had warned about the complex machinery of the Mills requiring careful maintenance and specialized knowledge. She wondered if this lost miners' rebellion had faced similar practical challenges beneath the weight of its ideals.

"Silence!" hissed a Security Committee member, glaring at them. The woman's face was gaunt except for a curious swelling along her jaw, a growth common among those who had worked the chemical vats in the Southern Mill. "Counter-revolutionary chatter endangers everyone."

The Craftsman fell quiet, but gave Eliza a meaningful glance.

Their passage was not without moments of terror. Twice they froze in silence as Palace Guard patrols passed overhead, their footsteps and voices filtering through cracks in the tunnel ceiling. A mother clapped her hand over her infant's mouth when it began to fuss, her eyes wide with panic. The baby's face turned an alarming shade of purple before the Guards moved on and the woman released her grip, sobbing silent apologies against the child's neck. Another time, a section of tunnel partially collapsed, requiring frantic but silent excavation to clear the path. The sound of shifting earth continued long after they'd passed, a reminder that the very ground beneath them remained unstable, revolution or no.

Most harrowing was the crossing beneath the royal checkpoint at Laboria's border. The tunnel narrowed to a crawlspace barely wide enough for an adult to squeeze through. Eliza felt the weight of earth pressing down, imagined the tons of soil and rock that separated them from air and light. Above them, Guard dogs barked and soldiers stamped their feet against the evening chill, unaware that dozens of "missing" workers were passing directly beneath them.

"If they discover this passage, they'll flood it," the Herald warned as they approached this section. Her voice contained the peculiar quality of someone who had imagined this scenario in detail. "No hesitation, no turning back. Keep moving forward no matter what you hear above."

Several hours into their journey, they reached a vertical shaft equipped with a crude rope-and-pulley system. One by one, they were hauled upward into the forest beyond Laboria's official boundary.

When Eliza and Lily finally emerged, the night air felt impossibly sweet after the stagnant tunnel atmosphere. Lily gulped it down in great greedy breaths, her face tilted toward the stars with an expression of wonder that briefly erased the premature adulthood revolutionary education had etched there.

They found themselves in a small clearing surrounded by ancient trees whose canopies blocked most of the moonlight. Eliza had never seen trees so large. In the controlled forests near Laboria, anything that reached a certain height was harvested for timber. These giants had never known the bite of Palace axes. Their bark was deeply furrowed, creating patterns like written language that no human had invented.

Other groups from different exit points were converging here, greeting each other with muted congratulations. Children were reunited with parents who had taken separate routes for safety. In total, nearly sixty workers and their families had made the escape. It was the first large-scale exodus of workers from Laboria since the kingdom's founding.

The Orator was waiting for them, standing on a fallen log to address the gathered escapees. Unlike his usual fiery rhetoric, he spoke with intimate warmth, welcoming them to "the first truly free territory of Laboria's workers." The red scarf around his neck seemed to absorb what little moonlight filtered through the canopy, creating the illusion that his head floated disembodied above the crowd.

"You have not fled," he assured them, his voice creating the rhythm that all had come to associate with revolutionary truth-telling. It was two short phrases, one long, repeat. "You have advanced! This is not retreat but the establishment of our forward position. From here, we will build the model of the society that will eventually transform all of Laboria."

A mother with a coughing child raised her hand tentatively. The child's cough had the wet, tearing quality that everyone recognized. Mill-lung started young. "My son needs warm shelter. How far to these caves we've heard about?"

The Orator smiled benevolently. "Comrade, your concern is everyone's concern now. The caves are less than an hour's walk, and our advance teams have prepared them with the most vulnerable in mind. Children and the elderly will have the warmest sections. Medical supplies, liberated from Palace Heights warehouses, await those in need."

The nervous tension that had gripped the group began to dissolve, replaced by cautious hope. The first step had been taken, and they had not been crushed immediately as so many feared. Of course, the Merchant King didn't yet know where they'd gone. The real test would come when he discovered not just their absence but their new location.

As they began the final leg of their journey toward the cave network, Lily looked up at her mother, her expression suddenly serious beyond her years.

"Are we revolutionaries now? Truly?"

Eliza studied her daughter's face in the dappled moonlight. The childishness still visible in the roundness of her cheeks contrasted with the calculating assessment in her eyes. "Yes, little one. There's no going back."

"Good," Lily nodded solemnly. "Teacher says revolutionaries make history instead of just suffering it."

The simple phrase, clearly memorized from revolutionary education, struck Eliza with unexpected force. They were indeed making history, for better or worse. The familiar miseries of the Gray Quarter had been exchanged for the unknown dangers of open rebellion. Whether this would lead to liberation or disaster remained to be seen, but one thing was certain. They had broken the Spell of Necessity that had kept Laboria's workers passive for generations.

As the trees thinned and the cave entrance came into view, its mouth illuminated by carefully placed lanterns, Eliza felt momentary exhilaration. The cave represented not just physical shelter but the concrete beginning of the world they had only theorized about in forest meetings. Here, beyond the Merchant King's reach, they would prove that workers could govern themselves, that prosperity could be shared equally, that cooperation could replace coercion.

Little did she know that this moment would represent the peak of revolutionary optimism. It was the brief, shining instant before theory met reality, and before liberation began its subtle, almost imperceptible transformation into a different kind of bondage.

***

By afternoon of the day following their departure, the co-incidence could no longer be denied. This was coordinated resistance. The Merchant King summoned his council in a fury, his jeweled fingers trembling as he clutched production reports. The gems, catching light from the tall windows, projected colored patterns across the parchment, red, blue, green, a rainbow of wealth that hadn't been earned but inherited and expanded through others' labor.

"Find these traitors! Every moment the looms stand idle costs my treasury a fortune!"

The captain of the Palace Guard bowed, his armor creaking with the motion. It was purely ceremonial armor, decorative etchings and gold inlay that had never seen combat, designed to intimidate through appearance rather than function. "We've already arrested family members for questioning, Your Prosperity. They claim ignorance, but a few nights in the dungeons should loosen—"

"Wait," interrupted the duchess who had previously voiced concerns. Her intervention was unprecedented. Women of the court rarely spoke during security discussions, and never to contradict Guard captains. "Arresting innocents may worsen the situation. Perhaps we should consider addressing some of their grievances? A small increase in rations might—"

Lord Puffinbottom gasped theatrically, his multiple chins quivering with indignation. "Negotiate with rebellious workers? What next! Inviting them to dine at our tables? Weakness invites revolution!"

The Merchant King silenced the debate with a raised hand. His rings clicked together, a sound that had accompanied royal decrees for generations, a soft metallic punctuation to commands that ruined lives. "Find the missing workers. Find whoever leads them. Make examples." His voice dropped to a whisper that somehow carried more threat than a shout. "And increase surveillance of any who show sympathy for these... collective ideas."

The duchess said nothing more, but that evening, she penned an anonymous note warning of the impending arrests and slipped it to her lady's maid, whose brother worked in the Mills. Her handwriting, usually flowing and elegant, became deliberately irregular, disguising its origin. The paper she used came from the kitchen rather than her personal stock, which might be traced. Small precautions that revealed larger doubts about the society she had previously accepted without question.

***

The first year in the caves became known later as "The Golden Year," though no gold existed in their modest community. The name referred instead to a rare period of genuine harmony and collective purpose. Systems established during initial planning functioned with surprising effectiveness, creating a stark contrast to the exploitation they'd fled.

The cave network proved more extensive than most had imagined, stretching deep into the mountainside with countless chambers and passages. Some areas showed signs of previous habitation, ancient hearths, crude drawings on walls, stone tools abandoned centuries ago. The advance teams had mapped the safest sections, marking dangerous passages with red cloth strips.

Daily life organized organically around a simple principle. From each according to ability, to each according to need. Every member contributed what they could, whether physical labor, specialized skills, or childcare. Distribution of resources, food, medicine, clothing, occurred through a transparent system overseen by rotating committees. No one went hungry, though portions remained modest by necessity.

Working groups formed based on expertise. Former Mill weavers established looms using salvaged materials. Hunters ventured daily into the forest, returning with small game and edible plants. Engineers who had maintained Mill machinery turned their attention to improving cave conditions, developing ventilation systems from scavenged materials and diverting a portion of an underground stream for drinking water. Healers who had secretly treated Mill injuries now practiced openly, combining traditional medicine with knowledge gleaned from stolen Palace Heights texts.

Morning assemblies featured reports from each work team, collective problem-solving, and revolutionary songs that echoed through the cave system. The acoustics transformed even untrained voices into something hauntingly beautiful, a chorus that suggested transcendence even as it sang of material conditions. Children were integrated into age-appropriate tasks, primarily gathering safe mushroom varieties from cultivated cave sections and learning practical skills alongside revolutionary theory. Their small fingers were perfect for harvesting the delicate fungi that broke under adult hands, and they took pride in contributing tangibly to the community's survival.

For Eliza, the first weeks brought a liberation she had scarcely imagined possible. Her weaving skills made her an essential contributor to the textile group. But unlike Mill work, she controlled her own pace and hours. When Lily fell ill with a mild fever, Eliza simply informed her team and spent three days caring for her child without the terror of lost wages or dismissal that would have accompanied such absence in the Mills. The community continued her share of resources without question, demonstrating in practice the solidarity that had only been theoretical in whispered forest discussions.

Even the Security Committee, despite their perpetual vigilance and occasional heavy-handedness, functioned primarily as protection rather than internal control during this period. Their patrols focused outward, maintaining an early warning system against Palace Guard incursions. Their drills prepared everyone for emergency evacuation should their sanctuary be discovered. Their occasional gruffness seemed a reasonable response to the very real dangers surrounding their vulnerable experiment.

Most remarkable to Eliza was how quickly children adapted to the new environment. Within days, Lily had formed bonds with other children her age, creating elaborate games in the smaller cave tunnels and returning each evening with fantastical stories of underground adventures. Her cheeks gradually filled out as regular meals, even simple ones, replaced the semi-starvation of Gray Quarter life. The haunted look that had shadowed her eyes began to fade, replaced by a child's natural curiosity and joy.

The Orator during this period seemed precisely the leader they needed, working alongside everyone else, participating in rotation for less desirable tasks, consulting broadly before decisions, and maintaining the inspirational vision that had brought them here while adapting pragmatically to immediate challenges. He took meals with different groups each day, listening more than speaking, his impressive memory allowing him to address everyone by name and remember their particular concerns or contributions.

When a roof collapse injured three people in the eastern chamber, he was among the first to join the rescue team, emerging hours later covered in dust and sweat but helping carry the injured to the medical area. His personal quarters during this period were no more comfortable than anyone else's, a small alcove furnished with the same basic sleeping mat and storage chest allocated to each adult.

Not long into their cave life, a significant victory bolstered community morale. A small team led by the Herald returned from a scouting mission with unexpected bounty, a Palace Heights supply wagon they had hijacked by posing as Guards, its contents including preserved meats, dried fruits, medical supplies, and most precious of all, clean warm clothing for the coming winter. The Herald had orchestrated the interception with minimal violence. The wagon's original Guards were left bound and unharmed in the forest, their uniforms taken for future operations.

The distribution of these goods occurred with scrupulous fairness. Children and elderly received priority for warmer clothing. Medical supplies went directly to the healer's area for communal use. Food was carefully inventoried and incorporated into the general supply, with small portions of dried fruit allocated immediately as a celebration ration for everyone. No special allotments were made for leaders or those who had conducted the raid, a principle that earned widespread approval.

The Orator announced this achievement with enthusiastic pride during evening assembly, emphasizing not just the material gains but the symbolic victory. "The Palace Heights nobles believe themselves untouchable," he proclaimed, "yet we have reached into their protected supply chain and redirected resources to those who truly created them. Today, a wagon. Tomorrow, the Mills themselves."

The evening ended with impromptu dancing in the central cave, percussion created by wooden spoons against hollowed logs, flutes crafted from river reeds, and voices raised in songs forbidden in Laboria. Eliza noticed even the ever-vigilant Security Committee members relaxing briefly, some joining the dance while others smiled from the shadows. They were witnessing what they had fought for, a community of equals celebrating shared triumph.

As The Golden Year progressed, small-scale raids continued with remarkable success. The growing network of sympathizers remaining within Laboria provided intelligence on Guard movements and supply shipments. Teams intercepted medicines, tools, and occasionally weapons, each time returning without casualties and strengthening the settlement's sustainability.

Equally important were the propaganda victories. The Herald's network distributed accounts of cave life throughout Gray Quarter homes, describing the alternative being built beyond the Merchant King's reach. These weren't merely idealistic proclamations but practical details, regular meals, democratic decision-making, children learning useful skills instead of Mill operations, medicine distributed according to need rather than wealth. Each successful raid and report of sustainable community life brought new escapees, with small groups arriving weekly through the underground passages.

By the sixth month of their exile, the cave community had grown to nearly a hundred members. Physical conditions remained basic but steadily improved as collective knowledge expanded. Food supplies stayed adequate through combination of hunting, gathering, limited agriculture in hidden forest clearings, and strategic liberation of Palace Heights resources. Most importantly, the sense of shared purpose and genuine agency created a psychological liberation as profound as the physical escape from the Mills.

During these early months, it seemed The Book of Understanding's promises might actually be realized, a society without exploitation, where cooperation replaced coercion and collective wellbeing guided all decisions. Eliza, like many, experienced a hope so unfamiliar it was almost frightening in its intensity. The possibility that Lily might grow up in a world fundamentally different from the one that had crushed generations of Gray Quarter residents seemed suddenly, improbably, within reach.

***

As summer turned to autumn, bringing the first hints of winter chill to the forest, subtle changes began to appear in the cave settlement. These early warning signs were so small that most dismissed them as necessary adaptations rather than fundamental shifts in the community's character.

The first sign came during a community assembly in late autumn, when the Orator proposed changes to the decision-making structure. "As our numbers grow, our meetings stretch longer," he explained, voice resonant with practiced reason. "Some matters require quick action that cannot wait for full assembly."

His suggestion of delegating minor decisions to working group leaders seemed sensible. Few questioned it. After all, was it not wasteful to debate for hours which hunting grounds to utilize each day or how to allocate newly acquired thread?

The Pragmatic Craftsman was among the few who voiced concerns. "In my experience, small decisions compound into large consequences," he said, his calloused hands working a piece of metal even as he spoke. "When we separate those who decide from those who implement, we create the seeds of hierarchy."

The murmurs that followed his statement included both agreement and dismissal. The Herald, her practical experience with Palace guards lending weight to her words, supported his caution. "Perhaps we could try this arrangement for one lunar cycle, then revisit whether it serves all equally?"

The Orator nodded with apparent thoughtfulness. "A reasonable compromise, Comrade Herald. Your practical wisdom serves us well, as always."

But when the lunar cycle passed, no review occurred. Meetings grew shorter as more decisions had already been made by the time the community gathered. Information flowed increasingly in one direction, from leadership to workers, rather than the vibrant exchanges that had characterized early assemblies.

The second subtle change appeared in housing arrangements. What began as practical accommodations for certain needs gradually evolved into differentiated spaces. Families with small children were initially placed in more protected alcoves, a consideration few disputed. Hunters who needed early departures were assigned near exit tunnels, again a practical matter. Those working late shifts in food preparation were given quarters near the kitchens.

Yet somehow, over weeks and months, these practical arrangements clustered the Orator and his closest supporters in the deeper, warmer sections, their administrative needs requiring proximity to each other. When winter arrived in earnest, these differences became more noticeable, as those in outer chambers suffered more frequently from the cold and dampness.

The third early sign came in the education system. What began as practical skill-sharing evolved into a more structured program run by former teachers and others deemed ideologically advanced. Children still learned useful tasks but spent increasing time on revolutionary consciousness formation, first as enjoyable games, then gradually as more serious study.

When Lily turned thirteen, midway through their first year in exile, she celebrated with a small gathering of friends, their laughter echoing through the tunnels. Eliza watched her daughter's face, lit by a single precious candle, and saw authentic happiness. The premature adulthood that had begun to settle on her in the Gray Quarter had receded, replaced by a child's natural enthusiasm and curiosity.

"This is the first birthday I haven't been afraid," Lily confided later that night as Eliza tucked her into bed. "In the Quarter, I was always scared something would happen to you, and I'd be alone."

"And now?" Eliza asked, smoothing her daughter's hair.

"Now we have everyone," Lily said with simple certainty. "The collective protects us all."

Eliza smiled at her daughter's conviction, yet something in the phrasing tugged at her mind. It wasn't simply gratitude for community support but contained seedlings of a different belief, one where the collective superseded all other connections. Still, she dismissed her concern as paranoia born from years under the Merchant King's oppression.

As winter deepened, bringing with it new challenges of heating, food storage, and increasingly dangerous hunting conditions, more changes appeared. The rotation system that had distributed tasks equally gave way to specialized roles. This evolution seemed natural enough, as those with particular skills could contribute more effectively by focusing on their strengths. But it also created new divisions, as some tasks were deemed more essential than others.

By the end of winter, as the first anniversary of their exodus approached, a distinct pattern had emerged. The egalitarian community that had formed spontaneously was gradually developing structures that separated decision-makers from implementers, leaders from followers, essential from non-essential. None of these differences were codified or acknowledged openly. Indeed, the revolutionary language of equity and collective ownership continued to pervade all discussions.

But watching Lily return from her education sessions, Eliza noticed subtle changes in her vocabulary and perspective. "Teacher says our personal preferences must yield to collective necessity," she explained one evening when Eliza questioned her sudden disinterest in drawing, an activity she had previously loved. "Art without revolutionary purpose is bourgeois indulgence."

The phrase was clearly not Lily's own, but a recitation of something taught. Eliza felt a familiar chill, reminiscent of the indoctrination she had witnessed in the Gray Quarter schools, though draped now in revolutionary language rather than obedience to the Merchant King.

As the first winter gave way to spring, marking nearly a year since their escape, the community celebrated with a festival of renewal. The Orator delivered a stirring speech about their achievements, "a new society built on foundations of equity and mutual care." The gathering was joyful, with music, dance, and a feast prepared from the first spring harvests and a particularly successful raid on a Palace Heights supply caravan.

Yet Eliza couldn't help noticing that the Orator no longer ate among the people but at a separate table with his closest advisors. His clothing, while still simple, was somehow better fitting, cleaner, less worn than most. His voice had developed new cadences and rhythms that commanded attention rather than invited dialogue. He had begun to speak of himself in the third person when describing revolutionary leadership, "The Orator believes," rather than "I suggest."

These observations lodged in Eliza's mind like splinters, small enough to ignore but impossible to forget completely. They were harbingers of changes to come, the first cracks in the revolutionary facade that would eventually reveal a structure disturbingly similar to the one they had fled.

***

The changes began so slowly that most didn't notice them until they had already taken root. With the exception of a perceptive few like The Pragmatic Craftsman, who catalogued the subtle shifts with growing concern, the transformation occurred beneath the threshold of collective awareness.

The first deviation from pure egalitarianism appeared six months into their new society, presenting itself as a practical necessity rather than ideological shift. During an evening assembly, the Orator raised a seemingly reasonable proposal. "Our scouting and raiding parties face increasing danger as Palace Guards strengthen patrols. These crucial missions require consistent teams with specialized knowledge, not rotating volunteers with varying capabilities."

This marked the first permanent exemption from the rotation system that had previously distributed both desirable and undesirable tasks equally. Raiders and scouts, primarily young men close to the Orator, were now dedicated solely to these operations, excused from routine cave maintenance, food preparation, waste management, and other daily requirements. Their exemption was justified by the danger they faced and their irregular hours, arguments few could contest.

Initially, these specialized teams maintained the communal spirit, taking their meals with everyone else and living in standard accommodations. Yet small distinctions emerged. Their equipment needs received priority, better boots, warmer clothing, specialized tools, justified as operational necessities. They developed distinct mannerisms and vocabulary, an esprit de corps that subtly separated them from ordinary workers. They began sitting together during assemblies, their shared experiences creating a natural cohesion that gradually evolved into a faction.

Not long after, a second adjustment to the egalitarian system appeared, again framed as practical adaptation rather than hierarchical development. The Orator proposed establishing a Coordination Committee to handle increasingly complex logistics as the community grew.

"Each morning assembly now requires hours to address all concerns," he explained reasonably. "Small decisions delay necessary actions. A dedicated team can manage daily operations, freeing the community to focus on productive activities. All significant matters will still come to full assembly."

The committee initially consisted of seven members, elected by show of hands during assembly. The Orator was unanimously selected, along with six others representing different work groups. The democratic appearance of this process obscured a subtle consolidation of authority. The nominations came primarily from those already close to leadership, and the assembly's approval felt more ceremonial than deliberative.

Before long, the committee's temporary administrative convenience became the settlement's de facto governing body. Assemblies shifted from decision-making forums to information sessions where the committee presented actions already taken and plans already formulated. Participation evolved from active governance to passive acknowledgment, a transformation so gradual many didn't recognize the fundamental shift in their relationship to power.

The distribution system's evolution revealed similar patterns. The initial principle, equal shares adjusted only for children's smaller appetites and those performing physically demanding labor, gave way to increasingly complex allocation categories. The simple designation "according to need" became stratified through introduction of terms like "specialized revolutionary requirements" and "operational necessity adjustments."

Food preparation, originally rotated among all adults, became the permanent responsibility of a designated kitchen team, their work supervised by a former Mill cook who had once managed the exclusive Palace Heights bakery. This centralization made sense logistically, specialized knowledge improved meals and reduced waste, but it removed most members from direct participation in a fundamental aspect of community life.

The Orator's role transformed subtly as well. His personal chambers, initially identical to others, gradually acquired small improvements, a proper bed frame rather than floor mat, better lighting from additional lanterns, a desk and chair for revolutionary correspondence, a small private area for strategic meetings. Each addition seemed minor, justified by administrative necessity rather than personal privilege.

His schedule increasingly separated from common patterns. While others followed the standard rotation of work shifts, his days filled with coordination activities that took place in spaces ordinary members rarely entered. His meals, once taken communally, now often arrived via assistants who cited urgent matters preventing his presence. His accessibility, once his most admired quality, diminished behind layers of facilitators who determined which concerns warranted his attention.

Even his physical appearance shifted gradually. By the middle of the second year, the Orator's voice had gained a new resonance, his posture straightened, his gestures more commanding. The simple revolutionary garb he had worn during the escape had been replaced with a tailored uniform that, while still modest in appearance, was clearly of finer quality than common clothing. His hair, once as unkempt as everyone else's, was now neatly trimmed, his beard shaped with precision rather than necessity.

The community's successful raids continued, but their character evolved. Initial operations had focused on basic necessities, food, medicine, tools. By the second year, raids increasingly targeted Palace Heights luxuries, wines, preserved delicacies, finer textiles. These items rarely appeared in general distribution, their absence explained as strategic reserves or diplomatic resources for expanding revolutionary alliances.

Most concerning was the transformation of the Youth Education program. The initial curriculum had balanced practical skills, basic literacy, and age-appropriate explanations of revolutionary principles. By the third month, the emphasis shifted dramatically toward ideological indoctrination and loyalty development. Children spent increasing hours in revolutionary consciousness formation, memorizing passages from The Book of Understanding and learning to identify counter-revolutionary tendencies in carefully constructed scenarios.

Eliza noticed the changes in Lily as her thirteenth birthday passed and she approached fourteen. The carefree playfulness that had returned during their early cave life gradually diminished, replaced by a serious dedication to revolutionary education. Her drawings, once filled with imagination and color, now featured revolutionary symbols and slogans with disturbing frequency. Her vocabulary shifted to include adult political terms that seemed memorized rather than understood.

As winter gave way to spring in their second year of exile, the Youth Sentinels emerged as a specialized group of children selected for their revolutionary alertness. Their distinctive red caps made them immediately identifiable, and they moved through the cave system with surprising authority for their age. Their primary function, described as revolutionary consciousness protection, involved reporting ideological deviations among adults, particularly parents. Their observations were delivered directly to the Education Committee, with rewards granted for particularly significant reports.

Lily was recruited to this group as she approached her fourteenth birthday. She returned from education sessions one evening wearing the red cap with solemn pride, explaining to Eliza that she had been chosen for special revolutionary responsibility. The terms she used weren't childish approximations but precise recitations of adult language, suggesting direct instruction in what to say to resistant parents.

"I can help protect our revolution from hidden enemies," she explained with rehearsed earnestness. "Teacher says sometimes people pretend to support equity but secretly want special privileges. Even parents sometimes have counter-revolutionary thoughts they don't realize are wrong."

The implications chilled Eliza more than the perpetually damp cave air ever could. Her own child was being weaponized against her, trained to monitor for ideological impurity in the guise of revolutionary vigilance. The natural trust between parent and child was being systematically undermined, replaced with political calculation disguised as principle.

That same week, the first case of revolutionary rehabilitation occurred. A former Mill mechanic named Jarek had questioned the increasingly unequal distribution of raid spoils during a work group discussion. His comments weren't particularly radical, simple observations about certain goods disappearing into the Coordination Committee's section while standard rations diminished. Yet the next day, he was absent from assembly.

The Orator addressed his absence directly. "Comrade Jarek is undergoing a period of revolutionary reflection to correct his individualistic tendencies. His concerns about distribution reveal lingering Palace Heights mentality, focusing on personal consumption rather than collective advancement. He will rejoin us when his revolutionary consciousness has been properly realigned."

Jarek returned two weeks later, visibly thinner and distinctly subdued. Where he had once been outspoken and quick to laugh, he now spoke little and laughed not at all. When asked directly about his revolutionary reflection by former friends, he responded with phrases that seemed memorized rather than authentic. "I'm grateful for the opportunity to correct my counter-revolutionary tendencies. The leadership's wisdom helped me recognize my selfish individualism."

His rehabilitation had occurred in a previously unused section of caves, deep, perpetually damp chambers where constant dripping echoed from unseen sources and light penetrated poorly even with lanterns. These became known unofficially as the reflection caves, their very mention causing nervous glances and changed subjects.

By halfway through their second year after their escape from Laboria, the cave settlement had developed a distinct stratification system, not identical to Palace Heights class structure but similarly effective at concentrating resources and authority. The crucial difference was linguistic, inequity now cloaked itself in revolutionary terminology rather than aristocratic tradition. "Revolutionary necessity" replaced "noble privilege," but the material distinctions remained, even as all continued to proclaim their commitment to the collective.

One evening, Eliza encountered The Pragmatic Craftsman in a quiet corner of the central cave, where he was repairing a broken loom shuttle. His calloused hands worked the wood with practiced precision, his weathered face serious in concentration.

"Have you noticed the changes?" she asked quietly, keeping her voice casual in case others were listening.

The Craftman's hands never paused in their work, but his eyes flicked briefly to meet hers. "I've catalogued seventeen distinct shifts since our arrival," he replied. "The transition from shared meals to designated dining sections was perhaps the most telling."

"Why isn't anyone speaking up?" Eliza whispered.

"The same reason we didn't speak up in the Mills," he said, testing the shuttle's movement with his thumb. "Fear has different clothing now, but it's still fear. And those who do speak up, like Jarek, suddenly need 'rehabilitation.'"

"What can we do?"

The Craftsman passed her the repaired shuttle. "For now, we work. We watch. We remember what true freedom might look like. And we prepare for the day when others finally notice what we already see."

His words reminded Eliza of his cautions during their forest meetings before the exodus, when he had warned that revolutionary fervor couldn't replace technical expertise. As the cave looms grew increasingly unreliable without proper maintenance, his warnings seemed prophetic. The practical challenges he'd predicted were proving as formidable as the ideological ones.

His words remained with Eliza as she returned to her quarters, watching Lily sleep in her Youth Sentinel uniform, the red cap still clutched in her small hand. The revolution that had promised liberation now showed disturbing signs of becoming another form of control. Yet what alternatives existed? Return to the Merchant King's brutal exploitation? That door had closed forever when they fled. Their only path lay forward, but increasingly, forward seemed to bend back toward what they had escaped.

***

As they entered the third year of their exile, with Lily now fourteen and growing taller despite the limited rations, the Wall of Truth appeared, a slate board mounted near the central gathering area, initially intended for community announcements and work assignments. Gradually, a section emerged labeled Revolutionary Vigilance.

Small notes began to materialize there. No direct accusations at first, just questions, implications, and shadows of suspicion cast.

> *"Who removed extra mushrooms from storage on Tuesday night?"*
> *"Note Comrade Viktor's frequent absences from revolutionary singing."*
> *"Why does Comrade Michael ask so many questions about leadership decisions?"*

But it didn't take long for the outright accusations to begin.

> *"Comrade Matthew takes twice as long at water collection as others, is he meeting someone?"*
> *"Comrade Sophie speaks of her former life in Palace Heights service with insufficient bitterness, potential class sympathizer?"*

The notes were unsigned, allowing accusers to remain anonymous while the accused were publicly named. Those who found themselves on the Wall were expected to provide self-criticism at the next assembly by confessing real or imagined ideological failings, expressing gratitude for being corrected, pledging deeper revolutionary commitment. The ritual held an almost religious quality, with public confession followed by communal forgiveness, though the forgiven were never quite trusted again. Their names remained in the Security Committee's ledger, marked for ongoing revolutionary evaluation.

More disturbing still was how children were integrated into this surveillance system. The Youth Sentinels were encouraged to report any counter-revolutionary behaviors observed in their families. Lily received special commendation for noting that her mother had "expressed doubts about leadership resource allocation," a minor comment Eliza had made while braiding her daughter's hair one morning. The praise Lily received for this betrayal created a terrible conflict in the child, visible in how she now alternated between clinging to her mother and watching her with suspicious scrutiny.

That night, Eliza found Lily crying silently in their alcove, her small shoulders shaking with suppressed sobs.

"What's wrong, flower?" Eliza asked, immediately at her daughter's side.

Lily shook her head, refusing to look up. "Nothing. It's counter-revolutionary to cry over personal feelings."

"Lily," Eliza said gently, trying to turn her daughter's face toward her. "You can always tell me anything."

The girl's hair had grown dull in the cave's perpetual dimness. Her eyes, when she finally looked up, held an unsettling conflict.

"Teacher says I did well to report you," she whispered, her voice caught between pride and shame. "But it hurt you, didn't it?"

Eliza chose her words with extreme care, aware that today's conversation might be tomorrow's report. "The revolution wants us to be truthful about our observations. You did what you were taught."

"But your face looked sad when they called your name. I saw it."

"Sometimes growth causes pain," Eliza replied, using the revolutionary language Lily would recognize. "Even necessary change can be difficult."

Lily seemed to accept this, her young face relaxing slightly. "Teacher says family bonds must be transformed into revolutionary bonds. That loving just one person too much weakens the collective."

Eliza felt a cold weight settle in her stomach. Yet she forced herself to nod.

"The revolution teaches us many new ways of thinking," she said carefully. "But remember that revolutionary theory must always be tested against real experience. That's what The Book of Understanding teaches."

It was a dangerous statement, subtle encouragement for Lily to trust her own observations rather than blindly accepting revolutionary doctrine. But the girl was already slipping back into her Youth Sentinel persona, her moment of emotional vulnerability passing.

"We have a special meeting tomorrow," Lily said, her voice regaining its rehearsed certainty. "Teacher says we'll learn to recognize facial counter-revolution."

That night, Eliza lay awake long after Lily had fallen asleep, listening to the constant drip of water from the cave ceiling. The revolution had begun with real hope, with the promise of equity and shared prosperity. Yet in little more than two years, it had created new hierarchies, new forms of coercion, new mechanisms for controlling thought itself.

Most disturbing was how children were being transformed into instruments of this control. Lily's eyes, once bright with curiosity and affection, now constantly evaluated and assessed, applying revolutionary standards to every interaction. Her laughter, once spontaneous, now came only during approved revolutionary activities. Even her dreams seemed to have changed. She sometimes murmured revolutionary slogans in her sleep, her small hands making the gestures that accompanied loyalty pledges.

The revolution was stealing her daughter more completely than the Merchant King ever had.

***

The revolution's first major military action came early in the third year after the exodus, when a group of twenty rebels infiltrated back into Laboria to sabotage the Eastern Mill's primary power system. The Orator himself led this operation, his familiar face now disguised with mud and ash, his distinctive voice suppressed to a whisper. The raid was meticulously planned, with scouts mapping Guard rotations for weeks beforehand.

Under cover of a moonless night, the saboteurs entered through maintenance tunnels known only to workers. They moved with practiced silence, using hand signals developed during cave life. Inside, they sabotaged the Mill's central steam engine, the heart that drove all mechanical operations. The damage was subtle but devastating, calibration screws loosened just enough to cause catastrophic failure once full production pressure built, lubricant reservoirs contaminated with fine sand that would gradually destroy precision components, pressure release valves subtly altered to trigger at dangerous thresholds.

The brilliance of the sabotage lay in its delayed effect and ambiguous origin. By the time the engine failed spectacularly two days later, erupting in a deafening explosion of steam and metal that killed three Guards and injured dozens of workers, the saboteurs were long gone, and the cause appeared to be accidental failure rather than deliberate sabotage. Palace Heights' own negligent maintenance could be blamed, a propaganda victory beyond the practical disruption.

What the rebels couldn't have anticipated was the Merchant King's response. Rather than improving conditions to win back worker loyalty, he imposed brutal collective punishment. Each Gray Quarter section connected to the sabotaged Mill saw its rations cut by half. Workers were subjected to loyalty inspections conducted by Guards empowered to use any means necessary to extract information. Public executions resumed, a practice that had been suspended for a generation, with suspected sympathizers hanged from specially constructed platforms at Mill entrances. Workers were forced to pass these grim displays daily, the bodies left hanging until they began to decompose, crows circling overhead in terrible anticipation.

Most devastating was the Merchant King's order regarding children. Any family with a member suspected of joining the rebels had their children temporarily relocated to special dormitories for patriotic reeducation. These facilities, hastily constructed near the central palace, held hundreds of Gray Quarter children in barracks-like conditions. Parents received no information about their welfare beyond periodic form letters, obviously dictated rather than written by the children themselves, expressing gratitude for being rescued from traitorous influences.

News of these measures reached the cave settlement through the Herald's network of informants. The initial elation over the successful sabotage transformed into horror as rebels realized the consequences for those left behind. Parents who had participated in the raid were particularly devastated, collapsing in grief when they learned their children had been taken.

The Orator's response to this suffering revealed the growing callousness of revolutionary leadership.

"Regrettable but necessary sacrifices," he proclaimed during assembly, standing on his customary raised platform while those whose children had been taken huddled in misery below. "Revolutionary transformation requires painful separation from bourgeois sentimentality. Those children will either be returned when we achieve victory, or they will become martyrs to the cause that liberates all future generations."

The parents did not find comfort in these words. Their faces hardened with a new kind of resolve that had nothing to do with revolutionary fervor and everything to do with primal parental instinct. That night, three families disappeared from the caves, presumably attempting to return to

Laboria to recover their children, despite the near-certain death that awaited them if caught.

Rather than acknowledging this as a natural human response, the Orator declared it counter-revolutionary desertion. The morning assembly became a grim spectacle as he ordered the remaining family members of those who had left to stand before the community.

"Let these examples of ideological weakness strengthen our collective resolve," he thundered, his voice echoing off the cave walls as he circled the tearful relatives. "Those who abandon the revolution for personal concerns undermine our sacred mission. What is one child compared to the liberation of all children? What is one family against the creation of a society where all are family?"

A terrible silence followed his words. Eliza found herself holding her breath, grateful that Lily was at Youth Sentinel training and hadn't witnessed this display. The relatives stood with downcast eyes, their bodies rigid with the effort of controlling their emotions. To show grief now would be to confirm counter-revolutionary tendencies. To defend their departed family members would be to share their guilt.

"These compromised comrades will undergo revolutionary rehabilitation," the Orator finally announced. "Through purification of their individualist attachments, they may yet serve our collective purpose."

As the assembly disbanded, Eliza noticed The Pragmatic Craftsman standing at the cave's edge, his expression carefully blank. When their eyes met briefly, she recognized the same thought in his mind that existed in hers. The line between the Merchant King's cruelty and the revolution's "necessary measures" had grown disturbingly thin.

***

The successful Mill sabotage, despite its brutal consequences, emboldened the revolutionary leadership. Several months later, the Orator proposed a more ambitious operation, contaminating Palace Heights' exclusive water supply.

"The nobility remains untouched by our actions," he explained during a strategy session, now held in his private chambers rather than open assembly. "They continue their luxurious lives while workers suffer increased oppression. We must bring the revolution directly to their doorsteps."

Using intelligence from new arrivals, a specialized team infiltrated the royal water system that supplied Palace Heights exclusively. The water wasn't poisoned, a line the Orator claimed he wouldn't cross, but was contaminated with a mineral compound that caused severe gastrointestinal distress. For three days, Palace nobility, including the Merchant King himself, experienced the kind of physical suffering common in the Gray Quarter but previously unknown in their privileged world.

The psychological impact exceeded the physical. Palace Heights residents could no longer take for granted the safety of their most basic necessities. Guards were doubled around water supplies, food tasters employed at every noble table, and a general paranoia descended upon the ruling class. Some nobles quietly departed for country estates, weakening the Merchant King's court precisely when he needed unified support.

The success of this action bolstered the Orator's position within the settlement. Critics fell silent as his strategic acumen seemed validated. His inner circle expanded, now including a personal guard of six specially selected men who accompanied him everywhere, their expressions perpetually vigilant, hands never far from concealed weapons. His living quarters expanded again, absorbing adjacent cave sections previously used for communal gatherings. The symbolism was difficult to ignore, common space literally transformed into leadership privilege.

***

By the end of the third year after their escape, what had begun as a classless society had developed a rigid hierarchy more complex than the one they had fled. The most visible manifestation was the Revolutionary Housing Allocation system that replaced the original communal arrangements.

"Living spaces will be assigned according to revolutionary necessity," announced the Orator's chief lieutenant, standing before a newly erected board displaying a complex diagram of the cave network. His voice had none of the Orator's hypnotic cadence, just flat certainty with an undertone of threat. "Specialized functions require specialized conditions."

What followed was the division of the previously unified community into stratified zones with markedly different conditions. The deepest sections, those with natural heating from thermal vents, protection from drafts, and proximity to fresh water sources, were designated Strategic Planning and Leadership Quarters. The Orator and his inner circle relocated there immediately, their possessions carried by newly designated "logistics workers" whose previous specializations as skilled mill operators were conveniently forgotten.

Mid-level caves with reasonable conditions became Productive Revolutionary Housing for those with useful skills, engineers who could maintain equipment, nurses with medical knowledge, former Mill supervisors who understood production systems but had joined the revolution. Their alcoves had the benefit of some ventilation without the dampness that plagued the outer chambers, and stone platforms raised sleeping areas above the perpetually wet ground.

The outermost caves, damp, cold, and furthest from water and sanitation, became General Revolutionary Quarters for ordinary workers. These areas were further subdivided based on assessed revolutionary commitment, with the least desirable spaces assigned to those deemed insufficiently enthusiastic. The worst spots, where water dripped continuously from limestone formations overhead, went to those who had questioned the Orator's more extreme proposals in forest meetings. The connection wasn't explicitly stated, but the pattern was unmistakable.

Most telling was the creation of Rehabilitation Spaces, isolated pockets where those who questioned the new arrangements were sent for "revolutionary consciousness realignment." These spaces had no amenities whatsoever, and their occupants were required to earn their way back to

General Quarters through demonstrations of revolutionary orthodoxy. The cold was most severe here, creating a physical suffering that mirrored the psychological pressure to conform. Three days in these spaces typically produced either complete ideological surrender or illness severe enough to require the limited medical resources, which was a different kind of surrender.

The transformation extended to communal activities. Initially, meals had been prepared and consumed collectively, with all members taking turns in food preparation and everyone receiving equal portions. A new system emerged when the Revolutionary Leadership Dining Facility began to operate separately, its contents shielded from general view by newly hung tapestries woven by textile workers who no longer had equal access to the fruits of their labor. The General Revolutionary Refectory served increasingly meager portions of communal stew.

"The leadership's enhanced nutritional requirements reflect their greater revolutionary mental exertion," explained the new Food Distribution Coordinator when questioned. She wore a special red armband with gold thread, a detail Eliza noted silently. "Revolutionary science has determined that ideological labor requires specific caloric support."

The coordinator's face betrayed no irony as she delivered this explanation, though her own increasingly substantial frame contrasted markedly with the diminishing bodies of those receiving standard revolutionary nutrition. She had developed the habit of speaking while looking slightly above her listeners' heads, as though addressing some higher revolutionary principle rather than the actual humans before her.

Bathing facilities, previously shared on a rotational schedule, became stratified as well. The leadership area included a section where natural hot springs provided comfortable bathing. The general population was limited to cold-water basins with strict time and quantity limitations, one basin per eight people, water changed once daily regardless of how many had used it. Skin conditions proliferated, creating new demands on the medical resources that were increasingly reserved for essential revolutionary personnel.

Perhaps most insidious was how quickly the inhabitants normalized this new hierarchy. Workers who had raged against Palace Heights injustice now rationalized Leadership privileges as natural and necessary. The revolutionary language provided a framework that made the new stratification appear not just acceptable but virtuous, an example of revolutionary science properly allocating resources based on contribution to the collective good.

"It's not the same as Palace Heights," insisted a man who had once organized protests against the Merchant King's feasts. His ribs now showed through his skin while the Orator's girth expanded. "Leadership needs strength to fight our enemies. Their comfort serves all of us." His eyes, however, didn't quite meet Eliza's as he offered this justification, and his fingers traced patterns in the cave dust, an unconscious diagram of doubt.

***

Through these changes, Eliza maintained a careful neutrality, focusing on her work and protecting Lily as best she could. She volunteered for additional textile shifts, as the mindless repetition of weaving provided rare moments of privacy and time to think. The mechanical rhythm of the loom, a sound that had once represented her oppression in the Mills, now offered a strange comfort. Perhaps, she sometimes thought, because it was honest in its machination, unlike revolutionary rhetoric that concealed growing tyranny behind liberatory language.

Her greatest concern was Lily's transformation. The child's Youth Sentinel education had intensified, with daily sessions now extending late into the evening. She returned from these gatherings with vacant eyes and new slogans, her natural childish spontaneity increasingly replaced by stilted revolutionary phrases. She watched her mother constantly, evaluating her for ideological correctness. When Eliza attempted to tell traditional bedtime stories, Lily corrected them with officially approved revolutionary alternatives in which noble characters were always evil and collective action always triumphed through unwavering commitment.

Most heartbreaking was Lily's drawing. Once filled with colorful imagination, her artwork now consisted almost exclusively of revolutionary symbols and punishments for class enemies, rendered with a technical precision that suggested adult guidance. When Eliza found a drawing of what appeared to be herself labeled "potential thought-criminal" hidden among Lily's belongings, she realized the full horror of what was happening. The revolution was not merely re-shaping society. It was colonizing her child's mind, turning Lily into both victim and instrument of the new oppression.

One evening, returning exhausted from a twelve-hour shift processing hides for winter clothing, Eliza passed the leadership section of the caves. The neatly woven tapes-try that usually covered the entrance had been careless-ly pushed aside, creating a gap just wide enough to see through. Through this opening, she glimpsed a scene that stopped her in her tracks, the Orator and several Committee members enjoying a private feast featuring bread, preserved meats, and wine. These items were officially classified as critically limited resources that ordinary workers hadn't tasted since leaving the Gray Quarter.

Most shocking was the laughter, uninhibited, genuine pleasure of the kind never displayed in general assemblies. The Orator tilted his head back in mirth, his throat work-ing as he swallowed wine directly from a bottle. A female Committee member leaned against his shoulder with casual intimacy, her red robe fallen open to reveal a silk shift be-neath, silk that had certainly been woven in the Mills they had supposedly liberated from exploitation. Their comfort with each other suggested these private feasts were regular occurrences, not rare exceptions.

Later that night, when she mentioned this sight to her work team partner, careful to frame it as a question rather than criticism, the woman's face paled. Her eyes darted to the darkened corners of their work area, checking for listeners before she responded.

"Don't speak of such things," she whispered, her fingers nervously working the leather she was supposed to be cutting into winter boot pieces. "Marta from cooking detail noticed the same and asked about it during assembly. She's been sent to 'ideological rehabilitation' in the deep caves. They say she was spreading counter-revolutionary demoralization."

The deep caves. Everyone knew what that meant. The chambers where constant dripping drove occupants to the edge of madness. Where the air contained too little oxygen for comfort. Where no light penetrated except the single lantern carried by those who brought the minimal rations permitted to rehabilitating elements.

Eliza fell silent, but her mind raced with uncomfortable comparisons. The Special Committee's justifications for inequity sounded increasingly like the Merchant King's pronouncements about natural hierarchy and necessity of proper distribution according to station, merely draped in revolutionary language rather than royal decrees. The mechanisms were different, the aesthetics transformed, but the essential pattern remained, some ate while others watched.

Yet what alternative existed? Return to Palace Heights oppression? Allow skepticism to undermine the revolution? These caves, despite their emerging problems, still offered more dignity than the Gray Quarter. Children still had enough to eat, if barely. The fever lily medicine remained available to all who needed it, though the definition of "need" was becoming increasingly selective.

Perhaps, Eliza thought as she prepared for bed in their small cave alcove, these were merely growing pains of a system finding its balance. Perhaps once the revolution succeeded in transforming all of Laboria, true equity would become possible. Perhaps the current leaders, with their private feasts and silken robes, would grow beyond their appetites once abundance was secured for all.

She watched Lily sleeping, the girl's face peaceful in ways it rarely was while awake and performing revolutionary consciousness. In sleep, the ideological mask melted away, revealing the simple child beneath. For that child, for all children, the revolution still promised something better than the Merchant King's calculated exploitation.

She couldn't know then how hope itself would become a resource carefully managed and distributed by revolutionary authorities, offered in just enough measure to maintain compliance while never quite materializing into promised reality.

***

Near the end of the third year of the settlement's existence, with Lily now nearly fifteen, a crucial turning point arrived. A major offensive was planned, simultaneous attacks on multiple Mills designed to cripple Laboria's production and demonstrate the revolution's growing power. The planning occurred exclusively within leadership circles, with ordinary members informed only of their specific tasks without understanding the larger strategy. Security measures intensified, with cave sections shut entirely to those not directly involved in planning.

In the weeks leading up to the operation, Eliza noticed unusual activities near the outer caves. Unfamiliar figures moved through the forest at odd hours. Small objects, possibly tracking markers, appeared and disappeared along rarely used paths. When she mentioned these observations to a Security Committee member, she was told dismissively that revolutionary operations required secrecy that she wouldn't understand. Her concern was noted with suspicious scrutiny rather than gratitude.

Two days before the offensive was to begin, the unthinkable happened. A Palace Guard raid struck the outer cave entrances at dawn, clearly guided by precise intelligence. The attack suggested intimate knowledge of guard rotations, defensive measures, and even the location of the Orator's private chambers. The invaders moved with certainty that could only come from internal betrayal.

The fighting was brutal but brief. The outer caves fell quickly, with guards capturing or killing dozens before the alarm could even spread to the inner chambers. Only the settlement's complex layout prevented complete disaster, as secondary escape tunnels allowed many to retreat further into the cave system and eventually to secondary forests camps established for precisely such emergencies.

In the chaos of evacuation, families were separated, possessions abandoned, and the wounded sometimes left behind when they couldn't be moved quickly enough. Eliza and Lily escaped through a narrow passage known only to water collection teams, crawling through mud as shouts and screams echoed behind them. Lily remained terrifyingly silent throughout their flight, her revolutionary training evident in her disciplined movement and absence of childish panic. Eliza found this unnatural calm more disturbing than tears would have been.

When the survivors regrouped at the forest camp that evening, accusations of treachery erupted immediately. The Security Committee began aggressive interrogations, focusing particularly on recent arrivals and those who had previously expressed doubts about leadership decisions. Three suspects were bound to trees, subjected to questioning methods indistinguishable from Palace Guard torture. Their screams carried through the forest, causing birds to scatter from branches in pulsing waves of panicked flight.

Rumors whispered that a recently arrived family, desperate for medicine for their sick infant still trapped in Laboria, had traded the settlement's location for promises of reunion and treatment. Others suggested that someone within the leadership itself had made a private deal with Palace Heights authorities. The truth remained elusive, but the atmosphere of suspicion and fear spread like poison through the displaced community.

The Orator, who had escaped with his personal guard intact, called for revolutionary justice against the traitor, though no conclusive evidence had emerged from the interrogations. Standing before the terrified survivors, his face illuminated by torchlight that deepened the shadows beneath his eyes and sharpened the increasingly authoritarian set of his jaw, he made a proclamation that would permanently alter the revolution's character.

"The setback we have experienced proves the necessity of absolute revolutionary discipline," he declared, his voice carrying none of its former warmth. "From this moment forward, all actions are governed by combat principles. Revolutionary military tribunals will replace community assemblies. Specialized revolutionary intelligence units will monitor for counter-revolutionary thought. Victory requires iron commitment beyond ordinary human sentiment."

That night, huddled with Lily beneath inadequate blankets as rain filtered through the forest canopy, Eliza finally confronted the truth she had been avoiding. The liberation they had sought had become a prison more insidious than the one they had escaped. The prison was not built with physical walls but with ideological ones, where captivity was disguised as freedom and dissent as treason. The revolution had inverted itself, recreating the very patterns of exploitation and control it had supposedly opposed, merely with new beneficiaries and victims.

The worst was the realization that no easy escape existed. Return to Palace Heights meant certain death. Speaking against the revolution's direction meant rehabilitation caves or worse. The path forward offered no clear hope, only the necessity of survival and protection of what remained human in herself and Lily amid forces that sought to transform them into mere cogs in the revolutionary machine.

As dawn broke through the trees, illuminating the makeshift camp where haggard survivors prepared for another day of revolutionary struggle, Eliza noticed something unexpected. The Pragmatic Craftsman sat alone at the edge of the clearing, fashioning a small wooden toy, a simple dancing figure moved by pulling a string. His face, though still bearing the marks of his rehabilitation, held a quiet determination as he worked the knife against the wood with practiced precision.

When he finished, he approached and wordlessly handed the toy to Lily. The girl hesitated, glancing toward the Youth Sentinel leader who watched with narrowed eyes from across the camp. Then, in a moment of recovered childhood, Lily reached for the toy, a real smile breaking through her revolutionary persona as the wooden figure danced in her hands.

The Craftsman met Eliza's gaze with subtle acknowledgment, a silent communication that beneath the revolutionary machinery, human connection endured. In that small act of creation and giving, he had demonstrated a form of resistance that even rehabilitation could not completely extinguish. It was not dramatic or violent resistance, but the simple insistence on humanity's essential nature, our capacity for generosity, creativity, and joy beyond ideological confines.

The revolution would continue its course, likely growing more oppressive as external threats and internal contradictions intensified. But within that inevitability existed small spaces of authentic human relation that no revolutionary doctrine could fully colonize. The challenge, Eliza realized, was not merely surviving physically but preserving these spaces of genuine humanity against systems, whether royal or revolutionary, that sought to exploit or extinguish them.

As the camp stirred to life, revolutionary slogans already filling the morning air, Lily carefully hid the wooden toy in her pocket. Her small act of concealment reflected a deeper truth, that true liberation might lie not in grand revolutionary transformations, but in protecting what made us human against all dogmas that would reshape us into their instruments, regardless of the banners they waved or the promises they made.

ACT IV

THE FALSE PARADISE

D AWN BROKE OVER LABORIA with an unsettling crimson hue. Tendrils of mist clung to the cobblestones as thousands of workers emerged from their homes and gathered in the central square of the Gray Quarter. Many carried hastily made red banners while others brandished tools of their trades as makeshift weapons. At their head stood the Orator, now wearing a red cloak adorned with golden thread.

"Requisitioned from a Palace Heights warehouse," he explained when asked about his new attire.

The morning air was electric with possibility. Eliza felt it too, a trembling in her hands that wasn't entirely fear. For once it was hope, dangerous and unfamiliar after years of careful hopelessness. She searched the crowd for Lily, now fifteen years old, finally spotting her among the Youth Sentinels. When their eyes met, Lily smiled a genuine smile that reminded Eliza of the child she'd been before revolution had touched their lives. In that moment Eliza allowed herself to believe that perhaps the sacrifices would prove worthwhile.

"Today," the Orator declared, his voice carrying across the assembled masses, "we reclaim what has always been ours! The Mills run by our hands shall be governed by our minds!"

The march to the Mills began with revolutionary songs and defiant chants. Workers who had spent lifetimes with downcast eyes now looked straight ahead, their faces alight with purpose. For many this day represented not just material hope but the restoration of dignity long denied.

The Palace Guards stationed at the Mills' entrance were fewer than expected. Most had deserted during the night, warned by relatives in the Gray Quarter that resistance would be futile. Those who remained surrendered quickly, more concerned with preserving their lives than the Merchant King's property.

As the enormous iron gates of the Central Mill swung open, the crowd erupted in jubilation. Workers rushed inside, embracing colleagues who had maintained the occupation strike through the night. Someone raised a red flag above the Mill's highest tower, visible even from Palace Heights.

Eliza found herself swept along by the tide of revolution, simultaneously exhilarated and terrified. This moment—the oppressed reclaiming the source of their oppression—was what they had fought for. Yet as she watched Revolutionary Enforcers round up Mill supervisors, binding their hands with red cord, she felt a hollow sensation in her chest.

"These class criminals will face Workers' Justice," announced a lieutenant as the supervisors were marched out to jeers and thrown debris. One supervisor, a middle-aged woman who had actually improved conditions in her section, protested, "I always treated workers fairly!"

A voice from the crowd shouted back. "There is no fair exploitation!" The woman was struck silent by a cudgel blow.

Eliza flinched, then glanced around quickly to see if anyone had noticed her reaction. Such involuntary empathy might be misinterpreted as counter-revolutionary sentiment. The thought itself, that she needed to hide her natural reactions, sent a whisper of unease through her celebration.

She searched for Lily amid the chaos but couldn't locate her daughter's brigade. The children had been given special revolutionary duties, she was told by a beaming Comrade. "Building the future begins with the youngest minds!"

***

The scene at the Royal Palace was one of panic. Servants fled with whatever valuables they could carry. The Royal Council met in emergency session, their customary pomposity evaporated like morning dew.

"The treasury is empty," reported Lord Puffinbottom, his fleshy jaw shuddering with fear. "His Prosperity transferred the gold to foreign banks last week."

"Where is His Prosperity?" demanded Lady Silkenpurse, clutching her jeweled necklace so tightly the chain cut into her flesh.

Their question was answered when a guard burst into the chamber. "The Merchant King's personal airship has departed! He's abandoned the palace!"

The councillors exchanged horrified glances, their lifetime of privilege suddenly offering no protection against the tide of history.

Within hours, The Collective's representatives arrived at the palace gates. There was no resistance.

In the central courtyard of Palace Heights, the Orator addressed the assembled workers, his voice trembling with emotion. Or perhaps with power.

"Comrades! Fellow laborers! Today marks the end of exploitation and the birth of the People's Republic of Laboria! No longer will the few feast while the many starve. No longer will labor serve capital. From this day forward, all Mills belong to those who work them, all palaces to those who built them!"

The crowd's roar was deafening. Workers rushed through the palace, marveling at its opulence, touching silk curtains and crystal chandeliers with calloused hands. Some began removing paintings and statues, declaring them the people's property now. Others discovered the wine cellars, and soon impromptu celebrations erupted across Palace Heights.

That evening, Eliza found Lily among a group of Youth Sentinels members being led through the former Royal Gardens. The teenagers moved in orderly lines, attentively listening to a Youth Coordinator describe how these once-private grounds would become collective recreation spaces. When Lily spotted her mother, she broke formation and ran to her, throwing her arms around Eliza's waist.

"We won, Mom!" she whispered, her voice vibrating with a joy Eliza hadn't heard in years. "The Merchant King is gone forever!"

Eliza smoothed her daughter's hair, noticing how it had grown past her shoulders again now that Mill work no longer required it to be kept dangerously short. "Yes, love. It seems we have."

"Teacher says I'll go to school now. Real school, not just Mill training. I'll learn everything! And we'll have enough to eat, and you won't have to work until you're sick anymore." Lily's words tumbled out in a rush of long-suppressed dreams.

Looking into her daughter's shining eyes, Eliza felt her own cautious hope bloom further. Perhaps the Old Scholar's warnings had been wrong. Perhaps this revolution could fulfill its promises without recreating the very systems it sought to destroy.

"Youth Sentinels Northstar Brigade, reassemble!" called the Coordinator, her voice friendly but firm. Lily gave her mother one last quick hug before running back to her line, her step lighter than Eliza had seen in years.

That night, sleeping on actual mattresses in a requisitioned Palace Heights residence, Eliza allowed herself something she had carefully rationed for years. Optimism. It tasted strange after so long without it.

***

The first months of the People's Republic were marked by exuberant celebration. Workers moved into Palace Heights mansions, marveling at indoor plumbing and heated floors. The contents of royal warehouses were distributed, providing many families with their first taste of luxury goods. Communal feasts were held in the palace gardens, with former servants now sitting alongside mill workers, all served equally from the royal kitchens.

Eliza was assigned a small but elegant room in what had been Lady Silkenpurse's manor. The irony wasn't lost on her. The woman who had justified worker suffering now likely suffered herself at the hands of the workers, if she hadn't escaped. Perhaps it was less irony than karma.

Yet the expected satisfaction didn't materialize. As Eliza lay on silk sheets listening to celebratory singing outside, she felt a growing emptiness. The weather had turned unseasonably cold, as if nature itself questioned the revolution's promise of perpetual spring.

This room, beautiful as it was with pale blue walls and ornate moldings, didn't feel like hers. No matter how many nights she slept here, she remained a visitor in someone else's life. Worse, she couldn't escape the knowledge that Lady Silkenpurse's servants—ordinary people doing what work they could find—had likely fled alongside their mistress, facing unknown hardships despite having committed no great crimes beyond serving the wealthy.

As she pulled the silk sheets tighter, Eliza realized that one spell had been replaced by another. The Merchant King's Spell of Necessity had kept workers believing they couldn't rise above their station. Now a new enchantment had taken hold, the Revolutionary Spell of Certainty, where questioning the new order became not just forbidden but unthinkable.

When Eliza mentioned these thoughts to Clara, her former Mill colleague and now residential reassignment coordinator, she received a worried look.

"Be careful with such sentiments," Clara whispered, glancing around though they were alone. "Sympathy for class enemies is being watched for. Revolutionary consciousness requires proper emotional alignment."

The warning, coming from a trusted friend, lodged in Eliza's thoughts like jagged glass. There was no room in this new world for nuance, for recognition of complex realities. She carefully composed her face into revolutionary certainty and changed the subject.

Lily had been taken to the newly established Youth Academy in the former Royal Military School. Parents were assured this was for their children's benefit, to protect them from counter-revolutionary influences and develop their revolutionary consciousness. Visits would be permitted once the children had adjusted to their revolutionary education.

When Eliza voiced concern about separation, a Young Sentinel coordinator smiled reassuringly. "Family attachment is natural but ultimately limiting. The revolution offers broader horizons."

The first permitted visit came three weeks later. Eliza arrived at the Academy, a severe stone building whose architectural grandeur now seemed vaguely threatening, clutching a small package of sweets she'd saved from her own rations. The entrance hall, once adorned with royal banners, now displayed enormous portraits of revolutionary heroes, the Orator's image largest among them. Children moved through the corridors in single-file lines, their voices raised in synchronized revolutionary songs.

Lily's appearance shocked Eliza. Her daughter had lost weight, and her eyes held a bright, feverish gleam. Her hair had been cut short again, in the revolutionary youth style that rendered all children nearly identical. But it was her manner that proved most unsettling, a stiff formality that replaced her natural exuberance.

"Greetings, Mother," Lily said, standing at attention rather than embracing Eliza. "I trust your revolutionary productivity has been optimal?"

Eliza struggled to hide her dismay. "I've missed you, Lily-flower," she said, using the childhood endearment deliberately, hoping to evoke the girl who had existed before.

Something flickered in Lily's eyes—recognition, perhaps even longing—but it disappeared quickly, submerged beneath practiced revolutionary composure. "Personal attachments are pre-revolutionary indulgences," she recited, though Eliza thought she detected uncertainty beneath the words. "Teacher says we must build connections to all workers, not just biological relations."

Their conversation continued in this vein, Lily alternating between revolutionary platitudes and occasional glimpses of her true self. When Eliza offered the saved sweets, Lily initially pushed them away, stating that "revolutionary nutrition requires no bourgeois extravagance." Yet moments later, when the supervising teacher briefly looked away, she snatched them and hid them in her pocket.

As their visit ended, Lily joined her classmates in a recitation of revolutionary pledges. During the performance, Eliza noticed her daughter watching her surreptitiously, gauging her reaction, seeking approval. She smiled encouragingly, and for just a moment, Lily smiled back, a genuine expression that cracked through her revolutionary persona before disappearing again.

Walking home, Eliza struggled with conflicting emotions. Horror at the systematic indoctrination of children. Fear for what Lily was becoming. Yet also hope from those brief moments where her true daughter had peeked through. Perhaps the revolutionary education wouldn't entirely extinguish the child she had raised.

***

Three months into the new society, Eliza noticed the Old Scholar's absence from the daily assemblies. His weathered face and careful contributions had become a reassuring presence amid the increasingly fervent revolutionary rhetoric.

"Where is Comrade Aldus?" she asked Clara during their work shift at the communal textile center. The looms here were smaller than the Mill's massive machines, but the rhythmic clacking still required them to lean close and speak softly.

Clara's hands faltered momentarily in their practiced motion. "Revolutionary Knowledge Alignment," she whispered, her eyes darting to check for nearby Sentinels. "They came for him three days ago."

A cold weight settled in Eliza's stomach. The phrase had become familiar in recent weeks—a euphemism for the disappearance of those who questioned revolutionary doctrine too persistently. "What happened?"

"The Educational Alignment session about the Northern Mill Protest." Clara's voice dropped further. "The coordinator claimed the workers demanded complete revolutionary control. Scholar Aldus corrected him. He said they only asked for small improvements and acknowledged the Merchant King's authority."

Eliza winced. She had been present at that session, had seen the dangerous stillness that came over the coordinator's face when the Old Scholar spoke up.

"He mentioned having original records," Clara continued, her fingers never stopping their work though her voice trembled slightly. "By the next morning, his name was on the Wall of Truth under Historical Saboteurs."

Later that evening, after checking that Lily was fully absorbed in her Young Sentinel training exercises, Eliza made her way to the Old Scholar's small dwelling. The door stood partially open, the interior in disarray. Three young Sentinels were methodically emptying his bookshelves, dropping volumes into large sacks marked Counter-Revolutionary Materials.

"Comrade, state your purpose," demanded the oldest, a boy no more than fourteen whose serious face was at odds with the childhood roundness he hadn't yet lost.

"I was told to collect his weaving supplies for redistribution," Eliza improvised, keeping her eyes appropriately lowered in the presence of revolutionary authority, despite it being embodied in children.

The young girl among them narrowed her eyes. "Weaving supplies should be processed through the Revolutionary Resource Allocation Office, not individual collection."

"New directive," Eliza replied, fighting to keep her voice steady. "Specialization efficiency. Direct transfer to production centers."

The children exchanged glances, their training in revolutionary procedure conflicting with the constant flow of new directives that even they couldn't keep pace with. Finally, the oldest nodded. "Proceed, but quickly. This dwelling will be sealed as a site of counter-revolutionary contamination once we've removed all dangerous materials."

Eliza moved carefully through the room, pretending to search for weaving supplies while actually noting what the Sentinels were taking. The Scholar's meticulous historical records, his hand-copied documents from before the revolution, the careful chronologies he had maintained—all were being stuffed into sacks without even being examined, branded dangerous by their mere existence.

On a small desk, she spotted a half-completed document. The top sheet bore the heading "Revolutionary Self-Criticism and Historical Realignment." Below it, in the Scholar's precise handwriting. "I, Aldus Tanner, confess to the counter-revolutionary act of historical distortion regarding the Northern Mill Protest. My bourgeois academic training led me to prioritize so-called 'factual accuracy' over revolutionary truth..."

The document continued with increasingly self-abasing admissions of "historical sabotage" and "memory crimes against revolutionary consciousness." Eliza recognized the formula from other public confessions she had witnessed. The words were too perfect, too aligned with revolutionary phraseology to have been written willingly by the thoughtful old man.

As she gathered a few balls of yarn and needles to maintain her pretense, Eliza spotted something partially concealed beneath the Scholar's bed. While the Sentinels were occupied with the bookshelves, she managed to slide it out with her foot and slip it into her bag—a small leather-bound volume with no title on its worn spine.

That night, concealed by the dim light of a single candle in her quarters, Eliza examined her find. It was a personal chronicle, the Scholar's private recording of events both before and during the revolution. Unlike the official histories, with their clear heroes and villains, absolute certainties and preordained outcomes, these pages contained observations full of nuance, contradiction, and human complexity.

One entry, dated just weeks before his arrest, caught her attention.

> "The revolution repeats a pattern I have observed
> throughout Laboria's history. What begins as gen-
> uine grievance transforms into absolutist certain-

*ty. What starts as liberation becomes new con-
straint. The Merchant King suppressed unfavor-
able information. The Revolution demands we actively falsify it. Both fear memory—the first because it might reveal alternatives to their rule, the
second because it exposes the gap between promise
and reality. Perhaps the most revolutionary act is
not fighting or seizing power, but simply remembering accurately."*

Eliza closed the book, her heart heavy. The Old Scholar
had seen what was happening with a clarity that arose from
historical perspective. While others, herself included, had
been caught up in revolutionary fervor or day-to-day survival, he had recognized patterns unfolding from his knowledge of the past.

***

In the Mills, workers hung red banners and elected production committees to oversee operations. The Book of
Understanding was read aloud during shifts, its proclamations about worker solidarity and collective ownership now
seemingly validated by reality. For the first time, workers
controlled the pace of production, scheduling reasonable
shifts with appropriate breaks.

Eliza, assigned to the textile division she knew so well,
initially felt genuine liberation in this new arrangement.
No more brutal quotas, no more penalties for bathroom

breaks, no more supervisors timing each movement with stopwatches. Workers shared knowledge freely, teaching each other specialized skills previously guarded by Guild hierarchies.

Food distribution during this period remained surprisingly efficient. The royal warehouses had contained substantial reserves—things they had never shared with the Gray Quarter during times of supposed scarcity—and these were now distributed through neighborhood councils. Many workers experienced true abundance for the first time in their lives.

The Orator, now officially titled First Representative of the People, spent these early weeks traveling between Mills and residential areas, personally overseeing the transition and addressing workers' concerns. His speeches retained their inspirational quality, focusing on the collective achievement and promising further improvements as revolutionary processes were refined.

"We have conquered political power," he declared during a mill assembly. "Now begins the greater challenge—creating a society where exploitation is impossible and prosperity is shared by all."

Eliza joined the applause, genuinely moved by these words that aligned with her deepest hopes. Yet even as her hands clapped, she noticed small details that troubled her. The Orator now traveled with armed guards who kept workers at a distance. His previously threadbare clothing had been replaced with finely tailored garments. He no longer ate communally but retired to private quarters after speeches.

The honeymoon period revealed how quickly certain patterns from the old regime reestablished themselves in new forms. The Orator's personal quarters in the former Royal Palace grew increasingly elaborate. His security detail expanded, creating distance between him and ordinary workers. Decision-making, initially conducted through open assemblies, gradually centralized in the newly formed People's Committee, whose members were theoretically elected but practically selected through carefully managed nominations.

Nevertheless, for this brief golden dawn of revolution, many workers genuinely believed that utopia had arrived. The nightmare of Mill exploitation seemed banished forever, replaced by worker control and material improvement. Even Eliza, despite her separation from Lily, found herself cautiously hopeful that the revolution might yet fulfill its original promises.

By the end of six months, subtle concerns began to emerge. The royal warehouses' bounty, distributed generously in the early months, proved finite. Production in the Mills had not yet returned to pre-revolutionary levels, creating the first hints of shortages in basic goods.

At the former Palace Heights, now renamed Victory Heights, the People's Committee established permanent headquarters in the most luxurious buildings. Committee members occupied entire mansions, justified as necessary for administrative efficiency and revolutionary security. While ordinary workers were assigned single rooms in subdivided noble houses, Committee leaders enjoyed full access to the amenities previously reserved for aristocrats.

The rationing system, initially introduced as a temporary measure to manage transition, became increasingly stratified. What began as simple distribution based on family size evolved into complex allocation categories determined by revolutionary contribution and ideological development. Committee members received leadership supplements justified as necessary for their demanding responsibilities.

Eliza noticed these patterns with growing unease. The revolutionary language might differ from aristocratic justifications, but the practical outcome looked increasingly similar—a small group enjoying abundance while the majority received diminishing shares.

One evening, returning from her shift, she passed the former Royal Dining Hall, now the People's Committee Administrative Canteen. The doors, usually kept closed during meals, had been left slightly ajar. Through the gap, she glimpsed a scene disturbingly reminiscent of pre-revolutionary Palace Heights. Committee members dining on multiple courses served by staff in clean uniforms, wine flowing freely, laughter echoing through the chamber. The next morning, she received her weekly ration, which included a smaller portion of gray bread, watery soup concentrate, and three withered potatoes.

"There have been necessary adjustments," explained the distribution worker, avoiding eye contact. "Temporary revolutionary sacrifice."

When Eliza visited Lily again at the Youth Academy, she found her daughter further transformed. The girl's movements had become mechanical, her speech increasingly dominated by revolutionary jargon. Yet Eliza still searched for, and occasionally found, moments when the real Lily emerged.

During one visit, as they walked through the Academy's memorial garden dedicated to revolutionary martyrs, Lily suddenly stopped before a small fountain. "I remember the rain," she said, her voice dropping to a whisper. "In the cottage, the roof leaked right above my bed. You used to put buckets to catch it, but sometimes in the night, they'd overflow and I'd wake up all wet."

The memory, mundane yet intimate, emerged unprompted by revolutionary context. Eliza's heart leapt at this evidence that her daughter still possessed memories untouched by indoctrination.

"You'd get so angry," Lily continued, a ghost of her old smile appearing. "Not at me, at the leaks. You'd yell at the ceiling like it could hear you."

"I did, didn't I?" Eliza laughed softly, reaching for her daughter's hand.

But as quickly as it had appeared, the moment vanished. Lily's posture stiffened again, and she pulled her hand away. "Teacher says we must eliminate counter-revolutionary nostalgia," she stated flatly. "The past was exploitation. Only revolutionary future matters."

A few moments passed.

"Are you fully committed to revolutionary transformation, Mom?" Lily asked when their supervisor briefly stepped away. The question carried an undercurrent of evaluation rather than childish curiosity.

"Of course," Eliza answered carefully. "I've always supported worker liberation."

"That's not the same thing," Lily replied with unsettling precision. "Teacher says many adults understand liberation but resist transformation. They want better conditions without changing themselves."

The visit ended with Lily reciting a revolutionary poem with her classmates, their voices blending in eerie harmony as they described the violent overthrow of parasitic exploiters in graphic detail. Eliza left deeply troubled by what was happening to her child's mind under revolutionary education.

Yet she clung to that brief moment by the fountain, evidence that beneath the revolutionary programming, her daughter still existed, like a small flame protected from wind.

In the Mills, the initial enthusiasm of worker control encountered practical challenges. The complex machinery that powered production required specialized knowledge to maintain, knowledge possessed primarily by engineers and supervisors who had been removed as class enemies. Production committees, composed of determined but untrained workers, struggled to maintain output levels.

"The machines resist revolutionary management," complained one committee member during a district assembly. "They seem designed to require bourgeois technical knowledge."

Rather than acknowledge the need for technical expertise regardless of class origin, the People's Committee introduced Revolutionary Production Science, a doctrine claiming that proper ideological alignment would overcome technical limitations. When production continued to falter, the explanation shifted to counter-revolutionary sabotage by hidden enemies.

The first public identification of such enemies occurred a few months later. Three former maintenance engineers were brought before a Workers' Justice Assembly, accused of deliberately withholding technical knowledge to undermine revolutionary production.

"We tried to explain the maintenance procedures," protested one engineer, his face already showing bruises from preliminary questioning. "But we were removed from our positions before we could train replacements."

The Assembly's verdict had been determined in advance. The engineers were found guilty and sentenced to revolutionary rehabilitation through productive labor in newly established work camps outside the city. This pattern would soon become familiar—technical failure reframed as ideological sabotage, followed by punishment of convenient scapegoats.

The verdict against the engineers sent ripples of fear through those with technical knowledge. Within days, whispers spread through the Mills of skilled workers disappearing in the night, leaving workstations abandoned with no explanation.

One evening after her shift, Eliza took a less traveled path home to avoid the Security Forces who had increased patrols following the trials. As she passed the abandoned workshop district, a shadow moved in a doorway. She froze, fearing guards, but instead found herself face to face with the Pragmatic Craftsman.

She hadn't seen him since the early revolutionary meetings. His face was leaner now, his hands even more calloused, but his eyes held the same steady practicality that had once earned him suspicion during ideological discussions.

"Eliza," he said quietly, nodding in recognition. "I hoped I might find you."

Eliza glanced around nervously before replying. "The Security Forces are searching for you. They say you've withheld technical knowledge."

"Yes," he replied with a bitter smile. "The crime of understanding how things actually work rather than how revolutionary theory says they should work." His fingers traced an invisible pattern in the air, the habit of someone who thinks through problems by building. "We're leaving tonight. A group of us. The eastern forests, beyond revolutionary territory."

"Who?" Eliza asked, though she could guess.

"Engineers. Mechanics. Those who saw what happened at the trial and know they'll be next. The Mills are failing not because of counter-revolutionary sabotage, but because machinery requires maintenance, skills require development, and systems require understanding. All things now labeled as bourgeois technical thinking."

He looked at her directly. "You should come with us. You've seen what this has become."

Eliza thought of Lily, embedded in revolutionary education. "I can't."

He nodded, understanding without explanation. "Your daughter."

"They've taken her," Eliza said simply.

"I know. Many parents face the same." He sighed, pulling a folded paper from his pocket. "If you change your mind, or when you need to, these markers will guide you to us. We're establishing something different. Not the Merchant King's exploitation, not the Orator's dogma. Something practical, where things work again."

The paper contained a simple map with subtle trail markings. Eliza tucked it into her shoe.

"Why risk coming back to warn me?" she asked.

"Because you listened. At the forest meetings, when I spoke of technical realities, you didn't dismiss me as a collaborator." His eyes held a seriousness beyond mere escape. "And because what we're building will need weavers too. People who create rather than destroy."

"What are you building out there?" Eliza asked.

For the first time, a genuine smile crossed his face. "We started with the basics. Shelter, clean water, sustainable food. But we're creating something larger—a community where skill and knowledge are valued without creating hierarchies. We've built workshops where craft is taught freely, gardens that feed everyone equally." He reached into his pocket and withdrew a small mechanical object—a miniature loom no bigger than his palm, intricately crafted from wood and metal scraps.

"One of our engineers made this for a child who wanted to learn weaving," he explained, demonstrating how the tiny shuttles still moved with perfect precision. "We have a school now, where children learn both practical skills and how to question everything they're taught. No revolutionary doctrine, no royal decrees—just a search for what works and what's true."

Eliza held the tiny loom, feeling its perfect balance. "And governance?"

"Those with expertise lead in their domains, but major decisions require consensus. We argue fiercely sometimes," he admitted with a slight laugh, "but no one disappears for disagreeing. It's messy, imperfect—but it works because it adapts rather than forcing reality to fit theory."

He glanced toward the distant Mills where lights still burned as workers struggled to meet impossible quotas with failing machinery. "When they purged the engineers, they believed revolutionary fervor would compensate for knowledge. Now the most complex machines are breaking down. Next will be the simpler ones. Eventually, even the basic systems—water, food distribution, sanitation. When that happens..."

His voice trailed off, the implication clear. The revolution was consuming itself, starting with those who understood how its physical infrastructure operated.

"How many have gone?" she asked.

"Enough to worry them, though they pretend otherwise. They erase us from photographs, claim the Mills are more efficient without us. But they can't erase the consequences of our absence." He pulled his worn cap lower. "I must go. The others are waiting."

As he turned to leave, Eliza caught his arm. "If things get worse..."

"The map," he reminded her. "Follow it when the time comes. We'll watch for you."

After he disappeared into the shadows, Eliza stood for a long moment. The Pragmatic Craftsman represented something the revolution couldn't tolerate, the stubborn reality that confronted ideological fantasy, the practical knowledge that couldn't be replaced by revolutionary fervor.

In the darkness of her room, Eliza made her first small act of resistance. Using scraps of fabric and thread saved from her work assignment, she created a tiny, secret record—a woven symbol of the path the Craftsman had shown her. She hid it beneath a loose floorboard, a physical reminder that alternatives existed beyond revolutionary territory.

For the first time since the revolution began, Eliza considered the possibility of escape. Not yet—not while Lily remained in the Youth Sentinels—but someday, when staying became more dangerous than fleeing. The thought itself felt like betrayal of revolutionary principles, yet also like the first breath after nearly drowning.

A few days after the Craftsman's departure, all Comrades were summoned to mandatory assemblies. The enormous screens installed throughout Laboria flickered to life with the Orator's face, now gaunt with revolutionary fervor, his eyes burning with an intensity that bordered on fever.

"Comrades of the People's Republic," he began, his voice carrying that hypnotic cadence that had once inspired hope but now sent shivers of dread through listeners. "We have uncovered a vast conspiracy against revolutionary progress!"

The camera pulled back to reveal a table covered with technical drawings, tools, and maps—items seized from the homes of the departed engineers and craftsmen.

"These so-called technical experts have revealed themselves as saboteurs of the highest order!" The Orator lifted a set of mechanical drawings. "These documents prove what we have long suspected. Bourgeois technical elements have been deliberately undermining Mill production while blaming revolutionary management!"

Eliza watched from the crowd, struck by how completely the narrative inverted reality. The drawings were standard Mill maintenance diagrams, created by the very engineers who had tried to train others before being removed from their positions.

"Their escape confirms their guilt," the Orator continued, his voice rising. "By fleeing collective accountability, they admit their counter-revolutionary activities!"

What followed was a masterclass in revolutionary reality manipulation. The Orator announced that production had already improved in the days since the "saboteurs" had fled. Mills that had been operating at thirty percent capacity were suddenly claimed to be exceeding pre-revolutionary outputs. Machinery that had sat idle for weeks due to breakdowns was declared operational through revolutionary technical initiative.

The Orator unveiled a new concept with theatrical flair. "Revolutionary Technical Consciousness."

"Bourgeois technical education is a lie designed to create false hierarchies of knowledge!" he proclaimed. "True revolutionary consciousness can overcome any technical challenge through collective will and ideological purity. We don't need their specialized skills—we need only proper revolutionary commitment!"

As proof, he introduced a series of Revolutionary Technical Heroes, ordinary workers with no previous mechanical experience who had supposedly solved complex engineering problems through revolutionary intuition. A teenage girl was celebrated for repairing a steam valve through application of revolutionary principles. An elderly man with no education had purportedly redesigned a failing gear system by thinking in accordance with The Book of Understanding.

None of these miracles had actually occurred, as Eliza knew from whispered reports of continued breakdowns throughout the Mills. But the assembled crowds applauded dutifully, fearful of being seen as lacking faith in revolutionary capabilities.

The response went beyond mere propaganda. By evening, new policies were implemented with brutal efficiency. All Comrades with technical training were required to register with the Committee for Revolutionary Technical Oversight, where their movements would be restricted and their activities closely monitored. Family members of those who had fled were reassigned to labor camps outside the city, their homes and possessions redistributed to ideologically advanced Comrades. New production quotas were established at levels even the fully functional Mills could never have achieved.

The People's Committee announced the formation of the Revolutionary Technical Purification Force, tasked with identifying "knowledge hoarders" who possessed technical skills they didn't share. Comrades were encouraged to report neighbors who repaired their own equipment or showed any sign of mechanical aptitude not immediately offered to revolutionary authorities.

"Knowledge privatization is counter-revolutionary theft," declared the new directive. "All skills belong to the collective."

The next morning, Mill workers arrived to find newly appointed Revolutionary Production Advisors at each station, young ideologues with no technical knowledge but absolute authority to enforce the new quotas. When machinery inevitably malfunctioned, these advisors blamed residual sabotage or counter-revolutionary resistance rather than acknowledging mechanical realities.

Within days, a special announcement proudly declared that three major machines in the Northern Mill had been revolutionarily recommissioned after being sabotaged by the traitors. Eliza later learned from a fellow worker that these machines had indeed been restarted and had catastrophically failed within hours, killing two workers and injuring fifteen others when a boiler exploded. The official report classified these deaths as "revolutionary martyrdom in the battle against technical sabotage."

In the former Royal Library, now the Center for Revolutionary Documentation, all technical manuals, engineering texts, and maintenance guides were removed from general access and placed in restricted sections accessible only to those with special authorization from the People's Committee. Knowledge that had once been freely available to Guild apprentices was now classified as potentially counter-revolutionary material requiring ideological contextualization.

The message crystallized with brutal clarity. Technical reality that contradicted revolutionary ideology was itself counter-revolutionary. The departed Craftsman and his colleagues hadn't simply left the revolution. In the Orator's new narrative, they had never truly been part of it, their expertise retroactively redefined as bourgeois contamination rather than valuable skill.

As production continued to deteriorate in the weeks that followed, the Orator's speeches increasingly focused on external enemies and internal saboteurs rather than the simple fact that complex machinery requires maintenance that revolutionary fervor cannot provide. Each breakdown became evidence not of technical necessity but of ideological impurity.

The revolution, confronted with the stubborn reality the Craftsman had warned about, chose to declare war on reality itself.

***

The People's Committee expanded its control to what the Orator termed the biological foundations of revolutionary consciousness. Alongside the purge of technical knowledge came a new initiative—the Revolutionary Birth Registry.

"The future of our revolution must be secured from its very origins," declared the Committee's newest proclamation. "Counter-revolutionary tendencies must be identified and corrected before they can contaminate revolutionary progress."

Once installed in the former Royal Administration Building, the Committee's Demographic Department began cataloging all pregnancies and births under the guise of ensuring proper revolutionary maternal support. The medical equipment, once maintained by the now-exiled technical workers, operated inconsistently, with frequent breakdowns blamed on "residual sabotage."

The decree appeared benevolent. Pregnant women would receive priority rations, specialized medical care, and reduced work assignments. New mothers would be provided with revolutionary child-rearing guidance to ensure their infants developed proper revolutionary consciousness from their first moments.

Behind this veneer of care lurked something far darker. Eliza discovered the program's true nature when her friend Marta, six months pregnant, received her first Revolutionary Maternal Evaluation.

The evaluation began with questions about the father's revolutionary status and the mother's family background going back three generations. Any connection to Palace Heights administrators, Guild masters, merchants, or—most recently added—technical knowledge hoarders immediately classified the pregnancy as Hereditary Risk Category.

"We've identified patterns of counter-revolutionary tendency in bloodlines," explained the clinical-voiced evaluator, whose medical training had been replaced by a few months of revolutionary consciousness alignment. "Genetic predisposition toward individualism requires enhanced revolutionary vigilance during developmental stages."

Pregnancies deemed high risk for counter-revolution- ary tendencies were subject to increased monitoring, with mothers required to attend daily consciousness alignment sessions where they listened to revolutionary doctrine through special amplifiers pressed against their abdomens. These devices, like much revolutionary technology, fre- quently malfunctioned without proper maintenance, some- times subjecting fetuses to hours of deafening revolutionary anthems.

"The revolutionary child begins formation before birth," the mothers were told. "Counter-revolutionary tendencies must be neutralized in utero."

After birth, infants underwent Revolutionary Aptitude Assessment—a pseudo-scientific evaluation of physical characteristics and reflexes supposedly indicating revolu- tionary potential. Those scoring highly received enhanced rations and priority placement in revolutionary childcare facilities. Those with "concerning indicators" were desig- nated for "special developmental intervention."

A chilling practice emerged regarding infants born with any physical imperfection or developmental concern. These children gradually disappeared from their families, trans- ferred to distant Specialized Revolutionary Development Centers from which few returned. The official explanation, that the collective would provide these children the ad- vanced care they required, contradicted whispered reports of neglect and experimentation in facilities now lacking qualified medical staff.

When Eliza saw Marta after her evaluation, her friend's face had aged years in days. Her hands trembled as she explained the invasive questioning, the judgments based on family history she couldn't control, the threatened separation from her child if she didn't demonstrate proper revolutionary alignment during pregnancy.

"They asked if I ever had counter-revolutionary thoughts," Marta whispered, her voice barely audible even in the privacy of her small room. "How can anyone answer that? Everyone has doubts sometimes. I lied, Eliza. I said I never questioned anything."

Eliza held her friend's hands, feeling the tremors of fear running through them. "You did what you had to do. For your baby."

"But what if they detect my lie? What if the baby cries too much and they decide it shows counter-revolutionary temperament?" Marta's eyes were wild with maternal terror. "The woman next door—her baby was taken last week. They said it showed physical indicators of bourgeois heritage. It was just born with a birthmark, Eliza. A birthmark."

The revolution that had once promised to liberate workers from exploitation now reached into the most intimate human experiences—pregnancy, birth, parenthood—imposing control more invasive than the Merchant King had ever attempted. This control became particularly cruel as it coincided with rapidly deteriorating prenatal care, as the medical equipment once maintained by purged technicians increasingly failed.

Through darkened streets patrolled by Revolutionary Security Forces, Eliza walked home wrapped in autumn's chill. A terrible realization struck her. Had Lily been born now, under revolutionary rule, she might have been classified

as developmentally concerning due to her early childhood illnesses. The fever that had nearly claimed her life
would have marked her for special intervention.

The thought sent bile rising in Eliza's throat.

***

Lily's transformation accelerated with her appointment
to the Red Fangs, an elite unit within the Young Sentinels
specifically tasked with administering revolutionary justice. Eliza learned of this not from Lily herself but from
a neighbor who congratulated her on her daughter's revolutionary advancement.

At their next permitted visit, Lily appeared in a special
crimson uniform with silver insignia that distinguished
Red Fangs from ordinary Young Sentinels. Her posture
was rigidly perfect, her gaze evaluative rather than warm.
She spoke of her new responsibilities with rehearsed
pride, describing how the Red Fangs directly enforced
revolutionary discipline against those identified as harboring counter-revolutionary tendencies.

"We're the revolution's surgeon," she explained, using
terminology clearly taught rather than intuited. "We remove ideological infections, to prevent the cancer from
spreading."

Yet even in this visit, Eliza found evidence that her
daughter wasn't completely transformed. As they walked
through the Academy's vegetable garden, carefully observed

by supervisors, Lily suddenly stooped to pick up a small stone, slipping it into her pocket with practiced discretion.

"What's that for?" Eliza asked quietly.

For a moment, Lily's revolutionary mask slipped, revealing a glimpse of the child beneath. "I collect them," she whispered. "Pretty ones. I hide them under my mattress." Her voice contained both guilt and defiance. Guilt at this counter-revolutionary individuality, defiance in preserving it anyway.

The stone was such a small thing, a tiny act of personal choice in a system that increasingly eliminated choice. This glimpse of her daughter's hidden humanity gave Eliza new resolve.

As they parted, Lily performed the formal Revolutionary Youth Salute expected at farewells. But as she turned away, she whispered, barely audibly. "I named my stone River." The childish confidence, shared furtively, told her mother that she still trusted her.

***

In the second year after liberation, Eliza joined the queue at the Victory District's communal distribution center. When she finally reached the front after three hours, the rations allocated to her were noticeably smaller than the previous week.

"There's been a temporary reduction," explained the distribution worker, avoiding eye contact. "Transitional difficulties."

The next day, a new proclamation appeared throughout the city, printed on the same presses that once produced The Book of Understanding. "Revolutionary discipline requires acceptance of necessary sacrifice. Those who complain about rations are objectively counter-revolutionary, regardless of subjective intent."

That evening at a community meeting, complaints about shortages were met with accusations of counter-revolutionary attitudes from Committee representatives. "Those who measure revolution by their stomach's fullness rather than society's transformation remain trapped in bourgeois thinking," declared a People's Committee speaker.

Then came a moment Eliza would replay in her mind for months. A thin man stood up, clearly starving but determined to speak.

"My children are hungry," he said simply. "The revolution promised food for all. Where is it?"

The meeting hall fell silent. Then the Committee representative smiled a terrible, cold expression.

"Comrade, identify yourself for the record."

The man hesitated, then squared his shoulders. "Albert Weaver, Northern Mill, Section Five."

"Thank you for your transparency, Comrade Albert. The People's Security Force will visit your residence tonight to discuss your concerns more... privately."

No one protested. No one met Albert's eyes as he sat down, ashen-faced. The next day, his family's quarters were reassigned to "more ideologically advanced Comrades." He himself was never seen again.

Shame burned through Eliza as she recalled how she had remained silent, how her fear had paralyzed her moral instinct to defend him. She had witnessed the beginning of a disappearance and done nothing, just as Gray Quarter residents had once looked away when Palace Guards took their neighbors.

The Herald, now working as a messenger between Mills, brought troubling reports to Eliza. Production had plummeted across all facilities. The weaving Mill where Eliza had once worked now produced barely a quarter of its previous output.

"The equipment keeps breaking down," the Herald explained during a furtive meeting in what had become a pattern of whispered conversations in shadowy corners. "The engineers and maintenance specialists who kept the complex machinery running, most were classified as management collaborators and removed from their positions. The revolutionary workers try, but without training..."

The Orator was forced to address these concerns in a speech broadcast from the former Royal Palace.

"Production challenges are the result of sabotage by counter-revolutionary elements still loyal to the deposed exploiter class," he declared. "The People's Security Force has established the Committee for Revolutionary Defense to identify these traitors among us."

The revolutionary leadership expanded the Wall of Truth, which had already become a fixture in neighborhoods, workplaces, and public squares. These boards, where Comrades were encouraged to post notices identifying counter-revolutionary behaviors, grew more extensive and invasive.

Like its previous iterations, these boards began with anonymous questions and insinuations before graduating to direct accusations with named targets.

> *"Comrade Nicholas takes long bathroom breaks during production hours. Avoiding revolutionary labor?"*

> *"Why does Comrade Reagan still possess jewelry from before the revolution. Hidden bourgeois attachment?"*

Those accused were expected to perform public self-criticism, acknowledging ideological failings and expressing gratitude for revolutionary correction. Failure to do so resulted in escalating consequences, from reduced rations to reassignment to labor camps established in former agricultural estates outside the city.

With each monthly visit, Eliza watched Lily climb higher in the Red Fangs' hierarchy. The timid pride of her early days in the crimson uniform had hardened into something colder, an efficiency that earned her rapid promotion. During this visit, Lily's uniform bore three new medallions, each representing a successful public judgment she had overseen.

"This one was for processing a hoarding network," Lily explained, touching a silver medallion shaped like a blade. Her voice contained none of the natural excitement a child might show when sharing accomplishments, just the flat satisfaction of revolutionary duty fulfilled. "Seventeen counter-revolutionaries identified and excised in a single operation. The Orator himself recognized my efficiency."

She pointed to another medal, smaller but more prominently displayed. "This one was for uncovering ideological contamination in the education sector."

"Who did you process for that one?" Eliza asked carefully, struggling to use the clinical revolutionary terminology.

"My former teacher," Lily replied without hesitation. "She was polluting young minds with counter-revolutionary materials, stories about kings and princesses where they weren't portrayed as exploiters."

Her finger moved to a third medal, bronze with a red enamel star. "And this was for production sabotage intervention. The neighbor from our old building, Mr. Carpenter. He undermined revolutionary morale by claiming machines worked better under the old system."

"And what happened to them?" Eliza asked, already knowing the answer.

"They were sent for revolutionary correction," Lily said with rehearsed certainty. "When their thinking is properly aligned with revolutionary truth, they'll return as better Comrades." Her hand unconsciously touched the blade insignia on her uniform collar—the symbol that distinguished Red Fangs from ordinary Young Sentinels.

The visit ended with Lily's supervisor returning to remind them that "family sentiment, while natural, remains secondary to revolutionary community." As Eliza embraced her daughter goodbye, she felt her daughter's body stiffen, maintaining revolutionary composure rather than yielding to maternal affection.

But just before they separated, in a moment when the supervisor looked away, Lily pressed something into Eliza's palm. Later, alone in her room, Eliza opened her hand to find a small stone, smooth, with flecks of mica that caught the light. River's sibling, perhaps.

***

A few months later, the first major public trial was held in the central square. Six people stood accused of "deliberately withholding technical knowledge to undermine the People's Revolution." Three were former Mill supervisors who protested that they had actually tried to provide training but were removed from their positions. The other three were technical workers accused of sabotage. All six were found guilty by the Committee for Revolutionary Defense.

The central square had been transformed overnight. Where merchants once sold bread and children played, a wooden platform now stood, freshly constructed of raw timber that would soon be stained. Above it loomed the massive screens that had been installed throughout the city to broadcast the Orator's speeches.

Today, they would serve a different purpose. Revolutionary Justice.

Attendance was mandatory. Security Forces checked names against district rosters, marking those absent for special attention. Eliza stood with her work unit, trying to control her trembling. This would be the first time the Red Fangs would actually carry out the punishments they'd been training for since their formation.

The crowd's murmur died as the Orator's amplified voice echoed across the square.

"Comrades of the People's Republic! Today we demonstrate the cost of betrayal!"

Six people were marched onto the platform, their hands bound with red rope, their faces bloated with bruises. Eliza recognized one, the baker who had once slipped extra bread to hungry children. His eyes, once kind, now stared vacantly ahead.

"These enemies have confessed to crimes against the revolution," announced the Orator. "They have admitted to deliberately sabotaging food production, hoarding resources, and spreading counter-revolutionary lies."

The impossibility of these charges hung in the air. The baker's small shop had been shut down months ago. How could he have sabotaged anything?

"But the revolution is merciful," continued the Orator. "We offer them the opportunity for redemption through public recognition of their crimes."

One by one, the prisoners were forced to the microphone. Each recited identical confessions in monotone voices, admitting to increasingly absurd acts of sabotage. Poisoning grain, destroying machinery they had never touched, conspiring with foreign powers that no one in the Gray Quarter had ever encountered.

The baker was last. When pushed to the microphone, he looked up, momentarily lucid. Instead of reciting his confession, he croaked.

"There is no food because the revolution has failed. Not because of sabotage. It has failed."

A collective gasp rippled through the crowd. The Orator's face darkened with rage.

"This," he snarled, "is what unrepentant counter-revolution looks like!"

The Red Fangs, twelve children in crimson uniforms, marched onto the platform. Their leader, a girl Lily's age, carried a gleaming blade.

The baker was forced to his knees.

"Revolutionary justice will be served by the future of the revolution," the Orator proclaimed.

The girl stepped forward, her face expressionless as she positioned the blade. The screens switched to close-up views from multiple angles, ensuring everyone could see. No one was permitted to look away. Security Forces watched the crowd, noting any who closed their eyes or turned their heads.

The sound that followed was worse than the sight.

A wet, thick thwuck. Then a brief, terrible silence.

The Orator's voice resonated through the square. "Comrades will now demonstrate revolutionary solidarity by approving this justice."

A Security Force officer raised his hand, initiating the applause. Slowly, terrified onlookers joined in, until the square echoed with forced applause for the horror they had witnessed. Those who clapped with insufficient enthusiasm were marked by observers positioned throughout the crowd.

As the applause continued, lasting precisely five minutes, the blood from the platform trickled down to the cobblestones, forming small rivulets that reached the feet of the front row of spectators. A woman fainted at the sight but was immediately propped up by Security Forces who ensured her hands continued clapping.

Eliza vomited until there was nothing left in her already empty stomach when she finally reached home. Beyond physical revulsion lay a deeper horror.

She had applauded. Like everyone else, she had applauded.

Her hands felt stained, though no actual blood had touched them. She scrubbed them raw in the small basin in her room, the sound of running water unable to drown out the memory of that terrible thwuck or the hollow percussion of forced applause that followed.

***

The weeks after the public executions brought unexpected new orders for Eliza. The Mills' decreasing output meant fewer weavers were needed, and she was reassigned to what the revolution called Cultural Production in the former Royal Library.

The massive building, now draped with red banners proclaiming Revolutionary Reality, housed hundreds of workers divided into specialized teams. Eliza's assignment revealed a sophisticated system with two equally important functions—revising the past and manufacturing the future.

"Comrade Eliza," her new supervisor explained, "your weaving expertise makes you ideal for our Historical Harmonization and Revolutionary Anticipation divisions."

The west wing housed revisionist teams modifying existing records. Here, Eliza altered commemorative tapestries and banners, removing purged officials from historical moments. As purges accelerated, she noticed a disturbing pattern. The photograph of the first red flag raised above the Mills—originally showing twenty revolutionaries—now contained only twelve. A month later, only eight remained.

"At this rate," whispered a fellow worker during a brief unmonitored moment, "soon the Orator will stand alone in every historical image."

The prediction proved correct. By the following month, Eliza was instructed to remove the final companions from key revolutionary imagery, leaving only the Orator as the revolution's sole architect and hero. Where once stood a collective leadership, now a single figure dominated every historical moment, as if the revolution had sprung solely from his mind and hands.

The east wing housed an equally important operation—the creation of anticipated reality. Here, Eliza joined teams fabricating evidence of revolutionary successes that hadn't yet occurred, and likely never would. She wove banners depicting bountiful harvests from fields that lay barren, created tapestries showing healthy, well-fed workers when the people were actually starving.

"Tomorrow's truth requires today's preparation," her supervisor explained, assigning Eliza to create commemorative images of a factory output milestone that production reports showed was mathematically impossible to achieve.

These fabrications worked in tandem with historical revisions in a system far beyond simple propaganda. As Eliza created imagery showing current grain yields at record levels, other workers modified historical production records to show pre-revolutionary yields as much lower. The same approach applied to everything. Housing conditions, healthcare, education, all depicted as vastly improved despite obvious deterioration.

"Reality must align with revolutionary vision," explained the Director during a mandatory lecture. "When reality falls short, it's not the vision that must change."

What made this system different from simple propaganda was its comprehensiveness. It didn't just control current information but systematically rewrote memory itself. The past wasn't merely censored but actively reconstructed to make the present seem inevitable and the future predetermined.

The fabricated future and revised past worked together to trap people in a false present. When promised prosperity failed to materialize, the failure was concealed by revising what had been promised. When current conditions deteriorated, historical records were modified to make things appear improved by comparison.

As weeks passed, Eliza noticed the Orator appearing increasingly alone in historical imagery. Photographs of the Mill liberation, once crowded with revolutionary leaders, now showed him standing alone, as if he single-handedly overthrew the Merchant King. Images of planning sessions now depicted him in solitary contemplation, all collaborators erased. Where committees had once made decisions, now a lone figure dominated every historical moment.

This visual transformation perfectly captured what the revolution had become. It was no longer a collective movement for liberation but the tyranny of one man, surrounded by empty space where Comrades once stood.

Each night in her quarters, Eliza made small acts of resistance. She created tiny private records of both the true past and the actual present—preserving images of those who had been erased and documenting the reality of current conditions. These contraband memories, hidden beneath a loose floorboard, became her rebellion against a system that sought to control not just actions, but perception itself.

In the Cultural Production facility, there was no room for individual thought or moral questioning. Workers who hesitated while removing purged figures or who failed to show sufficient enthusiasm when creating false futures quickly disappeared themselves, their names appearing on the next day's list of faces to be removed from history.

Eliza performed her assigned tasks with outward precision and revolutionary zeal, but each altered image, each fabricated success, only strengthened her private determination to preserve truth, however small, however hidden. The revolution could control public memory, but in the territory of her own mind, she maintained a stubborn resistance against the machinery of forgetting.

***

Almost two years after liberation, a new system was introduced as a Revolutionary Youth Vigilance Initiative. In reality, it was a nightmare of surveillance unlike anything Laboria had experienced under the Merchant King.

It began with the formation of the Expression Monitors, children selected from the Young Sentinels program and given special training in detecting facial counter-revolution. Unlike the Red Fangs who administered punishment, Expression Monitors focused solely on identifying ideological impurity through facial micro-expressions.

"Comrades with proper revolutionary consciousness have nothing to hide," declared the official statement as Expression Monitors were deployed to every workplace, housing block, and communal dining hall.

Each child Monitor carried a small notebook for documenting violations. They were trained to categorize expressions into approved and unapproved reactions.

> *Approved: fervent agreement, revolutionary enthusiasm, righteous anger at counter-revolutionaries*

> *Unapproved: doubt, fatigue, hunger, sorrow, neutrality*

When the Orator's speeches were broadcast on public screens, Monitors circulated through the crowd, studying faces. When news of agricultural "successes" was announced despite empty dining halls, they watched for signs of disbelief. When the names of newly discovered "traitors" were read, they noted whether viewers showed appropriate revolutionary outrage.

The first wave of arrests for facecrime bewildered the masses. People were taken for expressions they didn't even know they had made. A momentary furrow of the brow, a split-second tightening of the lips, all dutifully recorded by children whose observation skills were unnaturally enhanced through intensive training.

"Citizen #24601 has been re-assigned to agricultural rehabilitation for showing Class Three Facial Doubt during the Orator's speech on revolutionary prosperity," announced the community bulletin. When people were assigned to re-education, they were not only were stripped of the title of Comrade, but also had their entire identity erased. They could earn them back after acceptable behavior modification.

Soon people began practicing their expressions in any reflective surface they could find, polishing metal pots to mirror-like sheens, using still water in basins. Mothers taught children how to maintain revolutionary enthusiasm regardless of actual feelings.

"Think of something that makes you happy," Eliza overheard one mother instructing her son. "Then freeze that feeling on your face whenever an Expression Monitor is watching."

"But nothing makes me happy anymore," the boy replied.

The mother's expression remained fixed in a grotesque smile even as tears slid down her cheeks. "Then remember food. Remember what it was like to have enough food."

Children as young as eight developed an unnerving intensity of gaze, their natural playfulness replaced by constant vigilance. They moved through Laboria like small predators, hunting for the slightest facial betrayal. Their own expressions became mechanical masks of revolutionary perfection, as though their training had erased not just improper reactions but the capacity for genuine emotion itself.

Soon after, the Orator announced a new understanding of revolutionary science. Hunger, previously acknowledged as a temporary transitional challenge, was reframed entirely.

"Comrades," his voice boomed from the Screens placed throughout the former Gray Quarter, "our revolutionary physicians have made a remarkable discovery. What counter-revolutionaries call starvation is actually the physiological manifestation of ideological impurity!"

According to this new doctrine, truly revolutionary bodies required minimal sustenance. Those experiencing hunger were demonstrating their own counter-revolutionary nature, their bodies rejecting revolutionary transformation.

"The truly revolutionary Comrade," explained the Chief of Revolutionary Health, "directs physical energy to ideological advancement rather than selfish biological processes."

This obscene inversion of reality criminalized basic human needs. Comrades now had to hide their hunger as evidence of counter-revolutionary thought. Mothers pinched children who complained of empty stomachs, terrified that such complaints would mark the entire family for re-education.

The Orator's Office of Revolutionary Physiology introduced the hunger metrics in winter, when starvation had become too widespread to ignore yet too useful to solve. The revolution didn't try to feed its people, it simply redefined their suffering as revolutionary virtue. People competed to demonstrate their revolutionary commitment through self-destruction.

Overnight, posters appeared throughout Laboria displaying The Revolutionary Body Scale, anatomical diagrams showing seven stages of revolutionary physical development. Stage One showed a healthy body, labeled Counter-Revolutionary Physiological Excess. Stage Seven showed an emaciated figure with protruding bones, sunken eyes, and distended belly, labeled Revolutionary Physiological Perfection.

Comrades were required to report for monthly Physiological Alignment Assessments where their bodies were measured, photographed, and classified according to the scale. These evaluations were conducted publicly, requiring complete disrobing before Revolutionary Physiology Officers who documented each person's revolutionary progress.

During her assessment, standing naked and shivering in the cold evaluation hall alongside dozens of other women, Eliza experienced a moment of clarity so profound it nearly overcame her careful facial control. They had fought against the Merchant King because he had starved them, and now their liberation was defined by institutionalized starvation repackaged as virtue. The revolution had not eliminated suffering but sanctified it, transforming deprivation from misfortune to moral imperative.

The Officer measuring the circumference of her increasingly bony wrist nodded approvingly. "Excellent revolutionary progress, Comrade Eliza. Your body demonstrates commendable ideological commitment."

Eliza forced herself to smile, to express gratitude for this recognition, while her mind screamed at the obscenity of praising what was simply the physical manifestation of systemic failure. As she dressed afterward, her trembling fingers struggled with buttons that had grown loose on garments that once fit snugly, she caught sight of herself in the evaluation room's large mirror. The face that looked back was nearly unrecognizable. With hollow-cheeked and sunken-eyed, she was the physical embodiment of revolutionary success.

For a moment, she allowed herself to remember Lily as a small child, frighteningly thin during her illness, how Eliza had fought desperately to help her daughter gain weight, joining the revolution as the best option for food.

***

At the start of the third year, all Comrades were summoned to the central square again. The Orator—now addressing himself as "Guardian of Revolutionary Purity"—announced discovery of a vast counter-revolutionary conspiracy threatening the People's Republic.

"Enemies of the people have infiltrated our ranks!" he declared, his eyes blazing with righteous fury. "Former collaborators with the Merchant King, disguised as loyal revolutionaries, work to undermine our collective achievement! Only through revolutionary vigilance can we secure our future!"

Behind him stood a newly erected structure, the Wall of Revolutionary Justice, covered with thousands of names. "These citizens," the Orator announced, "require intensive re-education to align their thinking with revolutionary reality."

As the crowd strained to see if their names were listed, Eliza spotted her own halfway down the massive wall.

Beside it, carefully recorded by some faceless committee member, was her crime. "Harboring doubts about revolutionary methods."

Her heart seemed to stop, then restart with painful intensity. How had they known? Had her expressions betrayed her? Had someone reported her private comments? Or perhaps her careful preservation of true memories had somehow been discovered?

The thought she had carefully suppressed for years finally surfaced in her consciousness.

The liberation they had fought for had become a nightmare worse than the oppression it replaced.

The People's Republic of Laboria had not eliminated inequity. It had merely changed who decided who went hungry.

As Security Force officers moved through the crowd with their lists, Eliza made a decision that broke her heart but offered the only hope of survival. She would flee east, toward the forests, in search of the Pragmatic Craftsman and others who remembered what the revolution had originally promised.

She slipped away through a narrow alley, moving quickly but carefully to avoid the Security Force patrols. The sun was setting when she reached the outskirts of the city, where surveillance was thinner. There, in the shadow of an abandoned storehouse, a voice called out behind her.

"Mom?"

Eliza froze, then slowly turned. Lily stood there, her thin face unreadable beneath her red cap. Her Red Fang uniform was pristine despite the general deterioration around her, indicating her privileged status in the revolutionary hierarchy.

"You're leaving," the girl stated flatly. It wasn't a question.

"Lily, I—" Eliza began, but words failed her.

"Your name is on the wall," her daughter continued in the emotionless voice of the indoctrinated. "You harbor counter-revolutionary thoughts." She paused. Then added, "I reported you."

The betrayal struck Eliza like a physical blow. "You... reported me?"

"The revolution demands loyalty above family sentiment." Lily's voice recited the words mechanically, her eyes cold and evaluating. "Revolution requires the elimination of counter-revolutionary elements regardless of biological connection."

Eliza knelt to her daughter's level, though she dared not embrace her. "Lily, please. Come with me. There are people in the forest who have food, real food. We can be together, safe."

Something flickered in Lily's eyes. Not recognition or love, but an echo of calculation. Her left hand twitched slightly at her side, the same nervous movement she'd had as a small child when conflicted. She tilted her head, studying her mother with a gaze that wavered between revolutionary certainty and something more human.

"The Craftsman is still alive?" she asked, her voice dropping to a whisper that contained a hint of her childhood curiosity.

The question startled Eliza. "Yes. He's building something different out there."

"Real food?" Lily's voice cracked slightly, and Eliza caught a glimpse of how thin her daughter truly was, despite her privileged status. The revolution starved even its most devoted servants.

"And schools," Eliza continued, sensing a crack in the revolutionary armor. "Books that aren't just revolutionary texts. They've built workshops and gardens. People work together but they're still allowed to be... people."

For a brief moment, Lily's face softened, revealing the child beneath the revolutionary façade. Her eyes darted to the forest edge, visible as a dark line against the fading sky. But then her expression hardened again, revolutionary discipline reasserting itself.

"You're asking me to betray the revolution," she said, her voice taking on the precise enunciation she had learned in the Youth Academy. "That is a Category Three offense."

"I'm asking you to save yourself," Eliza whispered. "To remember who you were before all this."

Lily's hand moved to the small whistle at her neck, the signal device all Young Sentinels carried to summon Security Forces when encountering counter-revolutionary activity. Her fingers closed around it as her eyes remained fixed on her mother.

"The Young Sentinels assembly begins in six minutes," she said, her voice emotionless. "I will be missed if I don't attend. Security Forces monitor all approaches to the city perimeter."

She looked beyond Eliza to the forest, and for a heartbeat, something like longing crossed her face. Her hand trembled on the whistle. Then she reached into her pocket and withdrew a small stone – River, Eliza realized – and looked at it for a long moment, rubbing her thumb across its smooth surface as if seeking guidance.

"You have three minutes before I sound the alarm," Lily said finally, her voice carrying the peculiar cadence of recited doctrine. "Counter-revolutionary elements must be reported regardless of familial connection. Revolutionary duty supersedes biological sentiment."

The rehearsed phrases contrasted with the conflicted movements of her hands, still turning the stone over and over. Eliza understood that within the body that wore Lily's face, a battle was being fought between the revolution's instrument and the child she had raised.

"I love you," Eliza said simply, rising to her feet. "I will always love you, no matter what they make you do or say.

And if you ever find your way to the eastern forest, I'll be waiting."

The words seemed to bounce off Lily without penetrating, like rain against a sealed window. The child's expression didn't change, her revolutionary training holding firm against this counter-revolutionary emotional appeal.

"Two minutes," Lily stated, fingers still on her whistle.

With a final look at what remained of her daughter, Eliza turned and fled into the gathering darkness. Behind her, she heard the shrill sound of the Young Sentinel whistle cutting through the evening air, followed by the heavy footsteps of Security Forces responding to the signal.

***

As Eliza ran toward the eastern forest, tears blinding her path, she carried not just the physical pain of separation but the deeper anguish of knowing the revolution had turned the very children it claimed to liberate into instruments of their own continued oppression.

The true horror wasn't that the revolution had failed to create a better world. It was that it had succeeded in creating a world where betrayal became virtue, hunger became achievement, and love itself became counter-revolutionary sentiment to be purged from the new human it sought to forge.

And in that moment, as darkness closed around her and distant shouts indicated pursuit, Eliza understood the final terrible truth. The greatest spell wasn't the Merchant King's

Spell of Necessity that had kept workers compliant for generations. It was the revolutionary promise that liberation could come without replacing one form of tyranny with another more insidious still, a tyranny that claimed not just bodies but minds, not just labor but love, not just the present but memory itself.

The revolution's hollow victory was a utopia forcibly constructed from the ruins of human connection. But somewhere ahead in the darkness lay a different possibility—smaller, imperfect, but real. A place where looms still needed proper tension and mill wheels required specific water flow, where reality's stubbornness was not an enemy to be conquered but a teacher to be heeded.

As she reached the forest's edge, she paused to catch her breath against a twisted oak. Through gaps in the branches, she could just make out distant lights deeper in the forest. It wasn't the harsh glare of revolutionary searchlights, but the warm glow of lanterns hanging from the eaves of modest houses.

She had found the Pragmatic Craftsman's community.

ACT V

THE BROKEN KINGDOM

A S ELIZA REACHED THE forest's edge, the distant shouts of Security Forces grew fainter behind her. The shrill whistle of her daughter's betrayal still echoed in her ears. Her legs gave way as she stumbled into a small clearing at the outskirts of the settlement.

This, she thought bitterly, was the revolution's ultimate triumph. A mother forced to flee alone, separated from the child she had tried to save, running from the very society they had helped create.

Strong hands lifted her from the ground, voices murmured with concern rather than accusation. Through her fading consciousness, Eliza heard words that seemed to belong to another lifetime. "Get her to the doctor. Quickly."

She awoke days later in a wooden cabin, sunlight filtering through simple curtains made from hand-woven fabric. For a disorienting moment, she thought she had somehow traveled back in time, before the revolution, before everything changed. The room was modest but comfortable, a single bed with actual blankets, a small table with a vase of winter flowers, walls decorated with children's drawings that showed no revolutionary symbols or approved themes. The illusion shattered when she instinctively called out for Lily, only to be met with silence and the gentle restraining hand of a woman whose efficient movements marked her as a healer.

"Easy now," the woman said, her voice gentle yet authoritative. "You've been unconscious for three days. Severe malnutrition, exposure, and exhaustion. It's a miracle you survived."

"Where am I?" Eliza asked, her throat raw from disuse.

"Hope Creek," answered a familiar voice. The Pragmatic Craftsman stood in the doorway, his face more lined than she remembered but his eyes clear. Gray now dominated his once-brown beard, and a long scar ran along his left cheek, a mark of revolutionary "justice" that had somehow failed to kill him. "Welcome to what remains of freedom in Laboria."

Eliza struggled to sit up, her body protesting every movement. The healer supported her back, arranging pillows with practiced efficiency. "My daughter—"

The Craftsman's expression told her everything before he spoke. "You were alone when we found you."

"She's still there," Eliza whispered, the full weight of her loss crushing down on her. "She chose the revolution over me. She reported me."

The Craftsman sat beside her bed, his weathered hands gently taking hers. His palms were deeply calloused, bearing

the marks of practical work rather than the smooth soft-
ness that revolutionary leadership cultivated. "The Young
Sentinels' conditioning runs deep. It's not her choice. Not
really. They've been systematically transformed."

"She was going to sound the alarm," Eliza said, the words
feeling like stones in her mouth. "Her own mother, and she
was going to turn me in for 're-education,' which everyone
knows means torture or execution."

"What they do to the children is the revolution's greatest
crime," the Craftsman replied. "Not the food shortages or
the purges or even the public executions. It's how they
methodically destroy the natural bonds between parents
and children, replacing family loyalty with revolutionary
fervor. They've weaponized childhood itself."

Eliza turned her face to the wall, unable to bear the compassion in his eyes. She had failed in the most fundamental
duty of parenthood: protecting her child. Instead, she had
delivered Lily directly into the revolution's machinery of
indoctrination and watched as it stripped away her humanity piece by piece, replacing it with revolutionary certainty.

"I should have taken her and fled years ago," she whispered. "Before the Youth Academy, before the revolutionary education, before the Red Fangs. But I believed. I truly
believed the revolution would create something better."

"We all did," the Craftsman said quietly. "That's how it
begins, with genuine grievances and authentic hope. No
one joins a revolution expecting to create a nightmare.
But the seeds of totalitarianism are planted from the first
moment we decide that ideology matters more than humanity."

The healer interrupted gently. "She needs rest now. More talking tomorrow."

As the Craftsman rose to leave, Eliza caught his sleeve. "Is there any way to get her out? To bring her here?"

The sadness that crossed his face was answer enough, but he spoke the words anyway. "The Young Sentinels undergo extensive conditioning. Those who advance to leadership positions receive additional modifications. We've never successfully deprogrammed any of them. The few who escaped or were captured died rather than renounce revolutionary principles. Their identities have been systematically erased and replaced."

That night, alone in the small cabin, Eliza wept for the first time since her escape. The revolution had performed a kind of spiritual murder more absolute than physical death. At least the dead remained themselves in memory. Lily had been replaced by something that wore her face but contained none of her essential self.

***

As Eliza recovered her strength over the next weeks, Hope Creek revealed itself as an entirely different world from the People's Republic. The small settlement was nestled in a valley protected by natural barriers—steep ridges to the east and west, dense forest to the south, and a series of rapids and waterfalls to the north that made approach difficult. Clever camouflage and heat-dispersing systems concealed it from aerial observation, while an elaborate early warning network alerted residents to approaching patrols.

The settlement consisted of about two hundred people, including defectors from the revolution, escapees from re-education camps, and rural farmers who had fled forced collectivization. They had established a functioning community that defied revolutionary predictions of inevitable chaos without centralized control.

What struck Eliza most powerfully was the absence of fear. People spoke openly, voiced disagreements without looking over their shoulders, laughed without checking whether their humor was ideologically acceptable. Children played actual games rather than revolutionary development exercises, their faces animated by genuine joy rather than the strained enthusiasm of Young Sentinels performing approved activities.

"How long has this place existed?" Eliza asked the Craftsman as he showed her around the settlement. They walked slowly, accommodating her still-recovering strength, pausing frequently for her to catch her breath.

"Almost from the beginning of the revolution," he replied. "A handful of us recognized the direction things were taking when the first purges started. We established the initial camp with just twenty people. Others found their way here as conditions in Laboria deteriorated."

The contrast with the People's Republic was startling. While not luxurious by Palace Heights standards, Hope Creek residents appeared adequately fed and clothed. Work was hard but purposeful, directly connected to community needs rather than abstract revolutionary quotas. Small workshops produced goods as required, without the massive centralized Mills that had once been Laboria's pride.

"How do you survive?" Eliza asked, watching a group of weavers operating simple hand looms. "The People's Committee controls all the Mills, all the distribution networks."

"We abandoned their centralized model," he explained, pointing to smaller, modified production equipment. "Instead of one massive Mill, we built several smaller ones, each manageable by the people who actually use them. The textile workshop produces what we need, not what some committee demands. The same with our food. Individual families maintain their own plots but contribute a portion to community reserves."

They passed a school where children sat in a circle, listening to an elderly woman tell a story—an actual story with heroes and adventures, not the approved revolutionary narratives about class struggle and production victories. The children's faces showed genuine engagement, their questions spontaneous rather than rehearsed.

"No Young Sentinels here," the Craftsman noted, following her gaze. "Children are allowed to be children. We believe that's not counter-revolutionary but essentially human."

That evening, Eliza joined the community for dinner in the central meeting hall, a simple structure with a high roof supported by hand-hewn beams. Unlike the communal dining facilities in Laboria, where Comrades sat according to revolutionary classification and ate strictly rationed portions while revolutionary announcements blared from overhead speakers, Hope Creek's gathering was informal and organic. People sat where they wished, conversations flowed naturally, and food—simple but nourishing—was shared equally.

What Eliza loved most was the sound of genuine laughter. It wasn't the measured chuckles permitted for officially approved revolutionary humor, but spontaneous expressions of actual joy. A group of musicians played in one corner, their songs neither revolutionary anthems nor Palace Heights formal compositions, but folk melodies that spoke of love, loss, and resilience.

"We don't have much," said a woman who introduced herself as Marta, sliding onto the bench beside Eliza. Her face bore the characteristic scarring of a former dye worker, but her eyes held a brightness that had long since vanished from Laboria's Comrades. "But what we have, we share. And no one monitors our faces for 'counter-revolutionary expression' while we eat."

After dinner, as people lingered to talk or help clean up, the Craftsman introduced Eliza to the Council, seven residents elected by the community to coordinate essential functions. Unlike the People's Committee with its rigid hierarchy and revolutionary titles, these were ordinary people who continued their regular work while taking on additional responsibilities.

"We operate by consensus," explained an older woman who oversaw agricultural planning. "Disagreements are expected and respected. We've found that better solutions emerge from honest debate than from revolutionary certainty."

"And what about security?" Eliza asked. "The People's Republic won't simply allow an alternative to exist if they discover you."

"We maintain vigilance without paranoia," replied a former Security Force officer who had defected after witnessing one too many revolutionary adjustments of reality. "Everyone contributes to the warning network, and we have evacuation plans if needed. But we refuse to become what we fled. No internal surveillance, no loyalty tests, no revolutionary suspicion of neighbors."

As the meeting concluded, the Craftsman walked Eliza back to her cabin. The night was clear, stars visible in a way they never were in Laboria with its perpetual industrial haze. The air smelled of pine and clean snow rather than the chemical miasma of revolutionary production.

"Tomorrow," he said, "when you're feeling stronger, we'll talk about what role you might want here. Everyone contributes according to ability and interest, not revolutionary assignment."

Eliza nodded, too overwhelmed to speak. After years in the revolutionary machinery, the simple human decency of Hope Creek felt almost unreal. It was a dream from which she feared waking. Yet beneath this tentative appreciation lay the constant, gnawing ache of knowing her daughter remained trapped in revolutionary bondage.

That night, as on every night since her escape, Eliza's dreams were haunted by the same image: Lily in her Red Fangs uniform, her eyes cold as she denounced her mother. Each morning, Eliza woke with the same hollow ache, the knowledge that her child continued to exist physically while being erased spiritually, replaced by a revolutionary automaton in her daughter's form.

***

As the seasons turned, Eliza gradually integrated into Hope Creek's community. Her weaving skills proved valuable, and the familiar rhythm of working with threads provided a tenuous connection to her previous life. The Craftsman taught Eliza to operate the simplified looms his team had designed. His hands moved with remarkable precision, adjusting tension and alignment with intuitive understanding.

One day, as they worked, Eliza noticed a small frame on his workbench, partially hidden behind tools. Inside was a faded sketch of a woman with intelligent eyes and a determined expression.

"My wife, Jennifer," he said, catching her glance. "The most brilliant mechanical mind I ever knew."

Later, as they shared a simple meal in the community dining hall, he spoke again.

"She designed improvements to the Mill's steam system. When the revolution began, we joined together." His voice carried the controlled tone of someone who has practiced telling a painful story. "But when the Orator's plans became more extreme, Jennifer spoke up. She challenged the purges of 'technical collaborators,' argued that specialized knowledge wasn't inherently counter-revolutionary."

"They didn't listen," Eliza guessed.

"She became the first example. The Security Committee took her for 'revolutionary alignment.' When she didn't return, I demanded answers." The Craftsman's hands stilled. "The Orator explained their new understanding, that technical expertise was counter-revolutionary because it prioritized material constraints over revolutionary possibility."

His eyes met hers, carrying a shared understanding deeper than words. They had both lost someone to the revolution's hunger for absolute loyalty. The revolution had not merely taken their loved ones but had perverted the very values it claimed to uphold, transforming liberation into a new form of bondage more complete than any physical chains.

***

Refugees continued arriving at Hope Creek, each bringing news from within the People's Republic. Their accounts painted an increasingly grim picture of revolutionary failure. The Mills were collapsing, food production had plummeted, and revolutionary justice had become progressively more arbitrary and severe.

The reports about the Revolutionary Successor program that had evolved from the Young Sentinels painted a grim picture. These children, selected for their ideological fervor and severed completely from family connections, now served as the revolution's primary enforcement mechanism. Their absolute loyalty, untempered by human attachment, made them more effective than adult Security Forces in identifying and processing counter-revolutionary elements.

One evening, a new refugee arrived, a young man with haunted eyes who had served as a junior administrator in the Revolutionary Youth Program. After receiving medical attention for injuries sustained during his escape, he shared information at the community gathering that made Eliza's blood run cold.

"The Revolutionary Successor program has been reorganized," he explained, his voice hoarse from the journey. "They've created an elite tier they call the 'Vanguard Sentinels.' Only those showing complete ideological purity qualify. They undergo procedures."

"What kind of procedures?" asked a mother who had escaped with her children before they could be fully indoctrinated.

The young man's voice dropped. "A combination of things. The details are classified, but I processed the requisition forms. Crude surgeries to alter sensory pathways. Specialized drugs administered regularly to suppress emotional responses. Systematic isolation and sensory deprivation followed by revolutionary messaging. Sleep deprivation cycles with constant indoctrination. They've discovered that placing children in ice baths while reciting revolutionary doctrine creates a permanent association between physical pain and ideological deviation."

He looked around nervously before continuing. "Most disturbing are the procedures they call 'perceptual adjustments.' They strap the children to chairs with their eyes forced open, showing them images of family affection paired with painful stimuli, while pictures of revolutionary heroes provide the only relief. After months of this conditioning, the children physically recoil from displays of personal attachment and demonstrate an uncanny ability to detect the smallest signs of counter-revolutionary sentiment in others."

A murmur of horror ran through the gathering. Even in Hope Creek, where people had witnessed the worst of revolutionary excess, this represented a new level of atrocity. It was the systematic destruction of children's essential humanity in service to ideological perfection.

"Those who graduate from the program aren't the same children who entered," he added. "They've been hollowed out and rebuilt from the inside. Their conditioning is so complete that attempting to reverse it causes extreme physical distress. They can't disobey revolutionary principles without experiencing crippling pain—their bodies have been trained to punish independent thought."

Eliza's hands trembled as she forced herself to ask: "Do you know the names of those selected?"

"The most prominent is the one they call the First Child of District Three," he replied. "She was the youngest ever appointed to lead a Revolutionary Justice unit. Her dedication to revolutionary principles is considered exemplary. The Guardian himself presented her with the Revolutionary Vigilance Medal."

"Her name," Eliza pressed, already knowing the answer.

"Lily," he said. "Lily Shaw. They say she personally identified and processed over two hundred counter-revolutionary elements, including her own mother."

The room fell silent, all eyes turning to Eliza. She felt the familiar pain twist inside her, but kept her face composed through long practice. "She doesn't process her own mother," she corrected quietly. "I escaped."

The refugee looked confused, then understanding dawned. "You're her—"

The Craftsman intervened. "That's enough questioning for tonight. We all need rest."

Later, as Eliza sat alone by the settlement's small stream, the Craftsman found her. He didn't speak immediately, simply sitting beside her on the moss-covered rocks. The water flowed past, constant yet ever-changing, indifferent to the human suffering it witnessed. From the nearby trees, a nightbird called. It was a sound forbidden in Laboria, where even nature had been subordinated to revolutionary necessity.

"I need to know more," Eliza finally said. "About what they've done to her."

"Are you certain? Some knowledge brings only pain."

"She's my daughter. Whatever they've made her into, I need to understand it."

The Craftsman sighed. "From what we've gathered, the modifications can be extensive. They enhance certain capabilities while suppressing others. Perception is heightened. They can detect minute facial expressions, voice stress patterns, even subtle changes in body temperature that might indicate 'counter-revolutionary thought.' But emotional capacity is deliberately reduced. They can't feel fear, hesitation, compassion, or anything that might interfere with revolutionary function."

"Is there any way to reverse it?" Eliza asked, already suspecting the answer.

"The physical modifications perhaps, with skilled doctors. But the psychological conditioning..." He hesitated, weighing truth against kindness. "We've never seen anyone fully recover from that level of indoctrination. We had one Sentinel here briefly, a boy who was injured during a patrol and separated from his unit. Our doctors treated him, but even with his injuries and our kindness, he attempted to report us the moment he regained consciousness. When prevented from doing so, he entered a state of distress so severe his systems began shutting down. He died still trying to complete his revolutionary duty."

Eliza looked out at the water flowing past, constant yet ever-changing. "She's still in there somewhere," she whispered. "She has to be."

The Craftsman's silence was answer enough.

Back in her cabin, Eliza removed the small photograph she kept hidden in the lining of her shoe. It was Lily at seven, before revolutionary education had fully taken hold, smiling with the unguarded joy of a child who still felt safe in the world. Her fingers traced the outline of her daughter's face, remembering the texture of her hair, the sound of her laughter, the way she would scrunch her nose when concentrating on a difficult task.

"I failed you," she whispered to the image. "I thought the revolution would give you a better world. Instead, it took you away completely."

***

Three months after Eliza's arrival at Hope Creek, an unexpected visitor brought news that shattered the community's relative peace. The Herald—once the messenger between revolutionary circles, now part of the resistance network—arrived breathless and travel-worn, carrying information too sensitive to trust to the usual channels.

"There's been a major development in the People's Republic," she announced once the community leaders gathered in the central meeting hall. Unlike the formal assemblies of the revolution with their rigid protocols and mandatory expressions of revolutionary enthusiasm, Hope Creek's gatherings remained informal, people sitting on benches arranged in circles, speaking as equals.

"The Guardian has initiated a new purge," the Herald continued, accepting a cup of hot tea with gratitude. Her face showed the strain of her journey, deep circles beneath her eyes, skin weather-beaten from traveling through forest paths in unseasonable cold. "But this one's different from the others. He's turning on the Revolutionary Successor program itself."

Eliza felt a chill that had nothing to do with the evening air. "Why?"

"Paranoia, most likely. The enhanced Sentinels are the only ones with the capability to detect deception in his own behavior. They know when he's lying about production quotas, food reserves, revolutionary victories. Their enhancements make them impossible to fool with the usual revolutionary distortions."

The Herald continued, explaining that the purge had begun with the arrest of several mid-level Successor administrators. The official charge was "counter-revolutionary infiltration," but everyone understood the real motivation: the Guardian eliminating potential threats to his absolute authority.

"There's more," the Herald said, her eyes finding Eliza's across the circle. "The most prominent Vanguard Sentinel—the First Child of District Three—has been placed under revolutionary surveillance. Rumors suggest she'll be the next target."

Eliza's voice felt distant to her own ears. "On what grounds?"

"Another Vanguard Sentinel named Petra has apparently discovered counter-revolutionary materials in her quarters." The Herald's tone made clear her skepticism. "The accusation seems fabricated. This Petra has long resented being second to Lily in the program. They've been rivals since their earliest training, with Petra consistently falling short of Lily's perfect revolutionary alignment. But in the current climate, accusation is effectively conviction."

"What exactly is she accused of?" asked the Craftsman.

"Possession of pre-revolutionary artifacts. Apparently, she had a collection of small stones with counter-revolutionary significance. And a journal containing questions about revolutionary policies." The Herald shook her head. "Anyone who knows the Vanguard Sentinels would recognize the absurdity. They're incapable of questioning revolutionary doctrine. It's hardwired into their modifications. And they certainly wouldn't keep written evidence if they did."

Eliza felt a peculiar tightness in her chest. Stones.

"When will they move against her?" Eliza asked, forcing her voice to remain steady.

"Within days. They're building the case carefully. The Guardian wants to make an example, show that no one, not even his most perfect revolutionary instrument, is beyond suspicion."

That night, Eliza made a decision that defied all logic but arose from something deeper than reason.

She would return to Laboria.

Not to save Lily—that was likely impossible—but to witness what would happen to her. Some primal part of her, the mother that remained beneath all the pain and betrayal, couldn't let her daughter face the end alone, even if Lily would never know she was there.

When she informed the Craftsman the next morning, he tried to dissuade her.

"It's suicide, Eliza. You're on every Security Force watch list. The moment you enter the city—"

"I won't enter as myself," she replied, her mind already calculating disguises, routes, timings. "The resistance has channels in and out. I've studied them while working in communications."

"Even if you reach the city undetected, what can you possibly accomplish?" He adjusted the bearing assembly he was repairing, his hands working automatically while his attention remained on her. "You can't save her. You know that, don't you?"

"I'm not going to save her," Eliza said, the admission a fresh wound. "I'm going to witness. Someone has to remember what really happened, not what the Department of Historical Accuracy will record. Someone has to know that Lily Shaw existed, Not just the Revolutionary Sentinel they created from her body, but the actual child who loved sunshine and stories and collected pretty stones."

The Craftsman recognized the resolve in her voice. After a long pause, he nodded. "I'll arrange transport to the outer checkpoint. After that, you'll be on your own."

Over the next two days, Hope Creek mobilized to support Eliza's mission. The community's disgust for revolutionary methods didn't extend to imposing decisions on its members, even when those decisions seemed dangerous or futile. Instead, they provided practical assistance. An elderly woman who had worked in textile coloring helped prepare disguise materials, former Security Force members shared details of checkpoint protocols, and the medical team assembled emergency supplies concealed in ordinary-looking containers.

On the morning of her departure, Eliza met with the documentation team. "If I don't return," she told them, "make sure the truth about all of this survives. Not just the revolution's failure, but how it happened."

"We will," promised the Old Scholar. "Memory itself has become revolutionary."

The Craftsman accompanied her to the valley's edge, where a guide waited to lead her through the forest paths to the outskirts of Laboria. As they said their goodbyes, he pressed something into her hand: a small wooden carving of a bird, its wings spread as if about to take flight.

"My sister carved these," he said. "Before the revolution took her for 're-education.' It's what freedom looks like—not perfect revolutionary alignment but the ability to chart your own course, even when that course leads away from safety."

Eliza tucked the carving into her inner pocket, next to the hidden photograph of Lily. "If I don't come back—"

"We'll remember you both," he promised.

***

One day later, Eliza entered Laboria disguised as a cleaning worker from the outer districts. Her hair had been cut short and dyed gray, her face aged with carefully applied lines, her stride altered to suggest joint problems common among those exposed to Mill chemicals. The identity papers provided by the resistance network identified her as a worker with a classification low enough to be virtually invisible to Security Forces.

What she found shocked her despite the reports. The city had deteriorated beyond recognition. Buildings crumbled from neglect, their once-solid structures now precarious arrangements of failing materials held together more by habit than structural integrity. Windows were patched with revolutionary propaganda posters rather than glass. Streets that had once bustled with market activity, even during the

Merchant King's oppressive reign, now stood nearly empty except for Security Force patrols and Comrades hurrying to complete revolutionary obligations.

The people themselves had changed most dramatically. They shuffled through streets with the characteristic gait of chronic malnutrition: small steps, hunched shoulders, eyes perpetually downcast to avoid attracting attention. Their clothes, despite revolutionary claims of textile abundance, hung in poorly repaired tatters. Their expressions carefully maintained blank neutrality that revealed nothing, risked nothing, hoped for nothing beyond surviving another day of revolutionary reality.

The once-bustling markets had been replaced by distribution centers where people queued for hours to receive rations that wouldn't sustain them. At one such center, Eliza watched a mother receive her family's allocation: a small portion of grayish bread, three withered root vegetables, and a packet of what the revolution called "protein supplement" but everyone knew was processed mill waste. The woman accepted this with the required revolutionary gratitude, her face showing precisely the degree of appreciation expected—not too enthusiastic, which might suggest previous counter-revolutionary dissatisfaction, but not too subdued, which could indicate insufficient revolutionary commitment.

Most disturbing were the public screens installed throughout the city, displaying continuous revolutionary messaging interspersed with announcements of counter-revolutionary elements discovered and processed. Comrades were required to stop and watch whenever these announcements played, their reactions monitored by Security Forces for signs of insufficient revolutionary enthusiasm.

"Comrade Daniel, District Two, has been identified harboring counter-revolutionary cognition," proclaimed one such announcement, accompanied by images of a gaunt man being led away by Revolutionary Successors. "Revolutionary justice has been applied to protect ideological purity. Comrades are reminded that improper thought leads to improper action. Report all ideological irregularities to your local Revolutionary Clarity Office."

Eliza made her way to the safe house, a small apartment above what had once been a bakery, now converted to a Revolutionary Literature Distribution Center. The building, like most in Laboria, had deteriorated significantly. Walls that had once been solid now showed cracks where revolutionary maintenance fell short of structural necessity. The stairs creaked ominously beneath her feet, the wood rotting from unrepaired leaks in the building's roof.

Her contact, an elderly woman who introduced herself only as Michelle, provided updated information on Lily's situation. Unlike the performative revolutionary adherence Eliza observed on the streets, the woman's manner changed completely once they were alone in the apartment's small back room, which had been swept for surveillance devices that morning.

"They've moved up the schedule," the woman whispered, her eyes constantly moving between the door and window despite the precautions. "The First Child will face Revolutionary Justice tomorrow at dawn. Central Square. Attendance is mandatory for all District Three residents."

"What exactly is she accused of?" Eliza asked, accepting a cup of thin tea, a luxury by current Laboria standards, where even basic provisions had become scarce.

"Officially, 'harboring counter-revolutionary materials and maintaining unauthorized communications with external elements.' But everyone knows it's because she's too effective. Her enhanced perception can identify lies, even the Guardian's lies. That makes her dangerous."

Eliza felt sick. The revolution's logic had reached its inevitable conclusion. Even perfect revolutionary instruments became threats when their capabilities revealed the contradictions in revolutionary reality. "And this Petra? The one who accused her?"

"Will likely take her position. She's less enhanced for perception, more for interrogation and enforcement. Less dangerous to leadership, more useful against the population." The old woman's face showed the careful neutrality of long-term survival under revolutionary scrutiny. "There are rumors she personally planted the evidence, a collection of small stones and a journal with counter-revolutionary questions. Absurd, of course. The Vanguard Sentinels are incapable of such deviations. Their modifications prevent it."

"The stones," Eliza said, unable to keep her voice steady. "Do you know anything about them?"

The woman gave her a curious look. "Only what filters through the underground. Apparently they were small, ordinary pebbles, but each had been assigned a name.

Counter-revolutionary sentimentality of the sort the First Child has efficiently eliminated in others. The contradiction made the evidence particularly damning."

Named stones. Something of her daughter had survived the revolutionary conditioning, the surgical modifications, the systematic destruction of her original self. Some fragment remained, preserved in this small, secret act of continued humanity.

That night, Eliza hardly slept. The thin mattress in the safe house felt like stone beneath her, but it wasn't physical discomfort that kept her awake. Her mind raced with memories of Lily—not the cold-eyed Young Sentinel who had reported her, but the child who had collected pretty stones, who had laughed at the shapes clouds made, who had once sobbed over a bird with a broken wing.

Where did that child go? Was she truly gone forever, erased by revolutionary conditioning and surgical modification? Or did some fragment remain, buried beneath layers of programming and enhancement, a small flame protected from revolutionary winds? The stones suggested the latter—a tiny, hidden corner of Lily's true self that had somehow survived all attempts to eradicate it.

As dawn approached, Eliza prepared for her most dangerous mission. The woman provided her with a small identification pin worn by cleaning staff assigned to Central Square, a position low enough to avoid scrutiny but with sufficient access to witness the proceedings. Eliza pinned it to her tattered coat, rehearsing in her mind the shuffling walk and downcast expression expected of people in her supposed classification.

"Remember," the woman warned as Eliza prepared to leave, "show exactly the right degree of revolutionary engagement. Too much enthusiasm will draw attention as inappropriate to your class designation. Too little will mark you as harboring counter-revolutionary sentiment. And whatever you witness, maintain revolutionary composure. The Vanguard Sentinels are specifically trained to detect emotional responses inconsistent with revolutionary expectations."

"I spent three years perfecting revolutionary expressions," Eliza replied. "I know how to hide my true feelings."

The old woman's eyes softened momentarily. "You knew her, didn't you? Before she became the First Child."

Eliza hesitated, then nodded. There was no point in lies between those who had already risked everything against revolutionary falsehood.

"Then I'm sorry," the woman said simply. "For what you're about to witness. Remember that whatever they've turned her into, it isn't your fault. None of us understood what the revolution would become until it was too late."

***

Dawn came too quickly. Eliza joined the streams of people moving toward Central Square, keeping her head down, shuffling with the precise mix of revolutionary compliance and physical exhaustion that characterized Laboria's remaining population. Security Forces checked identification at various checkpoints, but her papers passed inspection.

Still, each interaction made her heart pound painfully in her chest. Discovery would mean not just her own destruction but the compromise of the entire Hope Creek network.

The Central Square that had once bustled with market stalls and children's games had been transformed into a stage for revolutionary theater. A raised platform now dominated the center, surrounded by massive screens showing revolutionary symbols, the broken chain, the rising sun of revolutionary dawn, the stylized Mill that represented productive labor. The cobblestones, once worn smooth by generations of commerce and community, had been replaced with uniform revolutionary paving stones, each stamped with approved slogans that masses would read with every step: "Revolutionary Vigilance Guarantees Revolutionary Victory" and "The Collective Supersedes The Individual."

Comrades were directed to predetermined positions based on their district and revolutionary classification, creating concentric circles around the platform. The inner rings held those with highest revolutionary status, the outer rings those under suspicion or of lowest utility. Revolutionary Adherence Officers moved through the crowd, monitoring facial expressions and body language for signs of insufficient revolutionary commitment.

Eliza, with her worker classification, found herself in the middle rings, close enough to see the platform clearly but far enough to blend into the anonymous mass. Around her, people stood in silence, their faces carefully composed to show the precise degree of revolutionary solemnity required, not too eager, which might suggest enjoyment of others' punishment, but not too reluctant, which would indicate counter-revolutionary sympathy.

The physical proximity of so many bodies did nothing to alleviate the profound isolation Eliza felt. In pre-revolutionary Laboria, even amid poverty and exploitation, people had found ways to connect: a whispered joke, a sympathetic glance, the small solidarities of shared hardship. Now, each person stood alone even in the crowd, surrounded by potential informants, every human interaction filtered through revolutionary calculation.

At precisely 7:00, a hush fell over the already quiet crowd as the Guardian himself appeared on the platform. Tall and imposing in his revolutionary uniform, he had changed since Eliza last saw him. His face had hardened, lines of paranoia etched around his eyes, his formerly charismatic presence now radiating only cold authority. The man who had once spoken with passionate conviction about worker liberation now moved with the rigid precision of someone who trusts no one, his gaze constantly sweeping the crowd for signs of insufficient devotion.

"Comrades of the People's Republic," his voice boomed through amplifiers placed throughout the square. Unlike his earlier speeches that had flowed with natural rhythm, his words now emerged in carefully measured cadences, revolutionary linguistic patterns designed for maximum psychological impact. "Today we witness the price of betrayal from within our most trusted revolutionary institutions. The revolution requires constant vigilance, even against those who appear most dedicated to our cause."

Security Forces led a small procession onto the platform. First came officials from the Revolutionary Justice Committee, their faces showing the peculiar blank expression of those who had learned that survival required the elimination of all identifying personality traits. Then members of the Vanguard Sentinels in their distinctive black and red uniforms, each moving with the uncanny precision of the surgically enhanced. Among them walked Petra, her face showing the carefully controlled satisfaction of one whose ambitions were being fulfilled. Her eyes, modified like all Vanguard Sentinels, periodically scanned the crowd with mechanical rotations, searching for reactions that deviated from revolutionary expectations.

And then Eliza saw her.

Lily entered the platform in prisoner's gray, her hands bound with the red cord of revolutionary justice. Even at this distance, the changes in her were apparent. Her head had been partially shaved, revealing surgical scars along her temples and the base of her skull. Her movements had the unsettling precision of the enhanced, lacking natural human fluidity. Her eyes, while still physically identical to those Eliza had gazed into since infancy, now contained nothing of recognition, emotion, or doubt. They moved in the systematic scan patterns of the enhanced, methodically processing visual data without the natural focus shifts of human vision.

Yet despite the modifications, despite the revolutionary conditioning, she was still unmistakably Lily. The same slender frame, the same angular face that had always resembled her father's, the same determined set of her jaw that Eliza recognized from Lily's earliest attempts to walk, to read, to master any skill that challenged her. Beneath the revolutionary instruments they had grafted onto her body, some physical essence of her daughter remained.

The Guardian himself read the charges, emphasizing each for maximum effect:

"Lily Shaw, formerly First Child of District Three, stands accused of counter-revolutionary infiltration, unauthorized retention of pre-revolutionary materials, and intentional perception manipulation to conceal revolutionary failures."

The specifics followed—a journal supposedly discovered in her quarters containing questions about revolutionary policies, a hidden collection of stones with counter-revolutionary significance, communications equipment allegedly used to contact external enemies. Eliza recognized the fabrication instantly. The journal was a clumsy forgery. Lily had barely written even before her transformation. But the stone collection struck Eliza with painful recognition.

Throughout the reading of charges, Lily stood perfectly still, her enhanced physiology showing none of the stress responses an unmodified human would display. Her face remained composed, her breathing steady, her gaze fixed straight ahead. The perfect revolutionary instrument, even in her moment of condemnation.

"How do you respond to these charges?" the Guardian finally asked, his voice carrying the ritual cadence of revolutionary judgment.

"I acknowledge counter-revolutionary materials were found in my possession," Lily replied, her voice mechanical, lacking the natural variations of human speech. Even her

voice had been modified, stripped of the individual characteristics that had once made it recognizably hers. "I cannot
explain their presence. I accept the judgment of revolutionary justice."

The formula was familiar, the standard response of those
accused in revolutionary trials. No defense was permitted,
no investigation conducted. The accusation itself constitut-
ed proof and the only acceptable response was acknowledgment and acceptance.

The Guardian nodded, satisfied with this display of revolutionary discipline even in disgrace. "Before sentence is
carried out, do you wish to address your fellow revolutionaries with your final understanding?"

This too followed the established pattern. The condemned would recite their failures, affirm revolutionary
principles, and thank the system for identifying their
counter-revolutionary tendencies. It was the final performance required before revolutionary justice concluded.

Lily began the standard recitation, her voice maintaining
its mechanical precision: "I acknowledge my counter-revolutionary failure and accept revolutionary justice as necessary purification. My inadequacy represents the persistent
danger of individualist tendencies within collective revolutionary consciousness. All revolutionaries must maintain
vigilance against similar deviations..."

Eliza watched, her heart breaking anew at the sight of
her daughter. She was physically present but essentially
gone, replaced by revolutionary programming so complete it
functioned even as that programming condemned her. The
revolution had not merely taken Lily from her but had taken

Lily from herself, replacing her essential humanity with a mechanism that now participated in its own destruction.

As Lily continued the familiar revolutionary litany, something unexpected happened. A young mother in the crowd, standing not far from Eliza, pulled her small daughter close, turning the child's face away from the platform. It was a small gesture of protective instinct, the kind that would normally attract immediate reprimand from Security Forces.

Lily faltered mid-sentence.

The hesitation was slight, perhaps imperceptible to most observers. But to Eliza, who knew her daughter's every expression, it registered immediately. Something had disrupted the perfect flow of revolutionary programming.

Lily's enhanced eyes, designed to detect minute behavioral deviations, had caught the mother's protective gesture. For a moment—brief but unmistakable—confusion flickered across her face, disturbing the perfect revolutionary mask.

"I..." she continued, but the mechanical certainty had vanished from her voice. Her eyes remained fixed on the mother and child, as though trying to process something her enhanced perception recognized but her conditioned mind couldn't interpret.

The Guardian noted the deviation, his expression darkening. He gestured to the Vanguard Sentinels to proceed with the sentence, unwilling to allow this disruption to continue.

But Lily wasn't finished. As the Sentinels moved toward her, something extraordinary happened. She turned slightly, her enhanced gaze sweeping across the crowd—and for the briefest moment, her eyes met Eliza's.

There was no recognition, no dramatic realization. How could there be, with Eliza so disguised and Lily so transformed? Yet something in that random connection seemed to trigger a cascade within Lily's modified mind. Her eyes widened slightly, her head tilted in the characteristic gesture of enhanced perception analysis.

"I remember," she whispered, the words barely audible but picked up by the platform's microphones.

The crowd stirred uneasily. This deviation from the script was unprecedented. The Guardian signaled more urgently to the Sentinels, but they hesitated, unsure how to proceed when the First Child herself was breaking protocol.

Lily's next words emerged not in the flat affect of her conditioning but with a hint of the intonation she had used as a child, a ghost of her true self surfacing through layers of programming and modification.

"I remember now."

What exactly she remembered—her mother, her childhood, her humanity before revolutionary transformation—Eliza would never know. But the breakthrough was unmistakable. Something essential, something the revolution had tried to completely eradicate, had surfaced in those final moments.

The Guardian, recognizing the dangerous psychological contagion this represented, barked a direct order. The Vanguard Sentinels moved with enhanced speed, surrounding Lily.

Eliza wanted to scream, to rush forward, to somehow save her daughter in this moment of recovered humanity. But any movement would have been futile, resulting only in her own capture without changing Lily's fate. She stood frozen, tears streaming down her face, as revolutionary justice proceeded with mechanical efficiency.

It was over quickly.

As the crowds were dismissed, instructed to return to their revolutionary duties with appropriate solemnity, Eliza remained rooted in place. Around her, people moved with the careful precision of those under constant surveillance, their faces showing exactly the degree of revolutionary sorrow permitted—not too much, which might suggest excessive attachment to an enemy of the people, but not too little, which might indicate counter-revolutionary callousness.

A Security Force officer approached, baton ready. "Comrade, return to your assigned duties immediately."

Eliza forced herself to move, to shamble away with the proper revolutionary deference. But inside, something had crystallized—a grief beyond tears, a clarity born of witnessing the revolution's final cruelty.

That night, Eliza made her way back through the resistance network, eventually reaching the forest beyond Laboria's boundaries. As she traveled toward Hope Creek, the reality of what she had witnessed settled into her bones. Lily was gone. Truly gone now, not just transformed but eliminated entirely. Yet paradoxically, in her final moments, Lily had been more present, more herself, than at any time since her revolutionary conversion.

"I remember now." The words echoed in Eliza's mind as she walked through the darkness.

It wasn't comfort, exactly. Nothing could comfort a mother who had lost her child twice. But it was something: a small flame of defiance against the system that claimed ownership not just of bodies and labor, but of memory and identity themselves.

When Eliza finally reached Hope Creek the next day, exhausted and grief-stricken, the Craftsman met her at the settlement's edge. His face showed no surprise at her return; he had known she would find a way to bear witness, no matter the cost.

"You saw?" he asked simply.

Eliza nodded, unable to find words for what she had witnessed.

"And was she... was there anything left of her?"

"At the end," Eliza whispered, "she remembered. I don't know what, exactly. But something broke through. She said, 'I remember now.'"

The Craftsman was silent for a long moment. Then he said quietly, "Perhaps that's the one thing the revolution truly fears. Not resistance or sabotage, but remembering. When people remember who they were before, what was possible, what was promised, that's when revolutionary control begins to crumble."

***

As the months went by in the hidden valley, Hope Creek continued to grow. New refugees arrived weekly, each bringing stories of worsening conditions in the People's Republic. The Mills had largely ceased functioning, food distribution had collapsed almost entirely, and revolutionary justice had become increasingly arbitrary as the Guardian struggled to maintain control over a failing system.

Among the refugees were children who had escaped revolutionary education before complete indoctrination. These children arrived traumatized, afraid to express natural emotions, conditioned to report counter-revolutionary tendencies in adults around them. Eliza found herself drawn to them, using her experience with Lily to help them recover their natural childhood. She taught them games without revolutionary messaging, read stories about children who were valued for their uniqueness rather than their conformity, and showed them it was safe to laugh, to cry, to question.

"Why don't you hate us?" asked one child who had been in the early stages of Young Sentinel training before his parents managed to escape with him. "I was learning to report people like you."

"Because it wasn't your choice," Eliza told him, the words opening fresh wounds even as they offered healing. "The revolution tried to turn children into weapons. That isn't your fault."

"Will I ever be normal?" the boy asked, his eyes showing the wary calculation of one trained to view human connection as a potential threat.

"You're already more normal than you realize," Eliza said gently. "The fact that you're asking that question shows the revolution didn't reach your core. The rest will come with time."

By the first snowfall, Eliza had established what the community called "Memory School," a place where children recovering from revolutionary education could relearn the human connections, individual creativity, and open questioning that revolution had tried to suppress. Unlike the Youth Academy with its rigid indoctrination, Memory School encouraged children to discover their own interests, develop their unique talents, and form authentic connections based on genuine affinity rather than revolutionary classification.

***

The following year, on the anniversary of Lily's execution, Eliza held a special ceremony. The entire community gathered at the small memorial garden they had established on a sunny hillside overlooking the valley. In the center stood a simple stone marker, inscribed with Lily's name and the words "I remember now."

Each person brought a small stone and placed it around the marker, creating a growing circle of memory. Unlike revolutionary ceremonies with their prescribed emotions and mechanical recitations, this gathering had no specific protocol. Some stood in silent reflection, others shared memories of their own lost children, still others spoke of what they hoped to rebuild in revolution's aftermath.

Eliza herself placed a special stone: one she had found in the stream near her cabin, with flecks of mica that caught the sunlight in dancing patterns. The kind Lily had once collected before revolutionary education taught her that beauty without purpose was counter-revolutionary indulgence.

"I thought for so long that I had failed you," she whispered to the memory of her daughter. "But even with everything they did to erase you, something essential remained. And in that, there's both terrible grief and unexpected hope."

The stone joined dozens of others, a growing monument. Unlike revolutionary monuments with their imposing size and absolutist messaging, this simple circle of stones represented something more modest yet ultimately more powerful: the refusal to forget.

***

The fairy tale had come full circle. The Spell of Necessity that had once kept workers passive under the Merchant King had been broken, only to be replaced by revolutionary enchantment more absolute in its demands. The Mills still stood, though now they produced little. The kingdom remained divided, though now between revolutionary truth and actual reality. And the children, for whom the revolution had supposedly been fought, had become its most tragic casualties.

Yet something remained that neither spell could fully capture—the possibility of genuine freedom, built not on perfect systems but on the recognition of imperfect humanity.

As Eliza stood watching the sun set over Hope Creek one evening, the Craftsman joined her on the hillside. Together they observed the small community below: people working, talking, disagreeing, connecting, all without revolutionary supervision or approved protocols.

"It's not perfect," the Craftsman said, nodding toward a heated discussion taking place near the central workshop. "People still argue. Resources are still limited. Problems still arise."

"But they're human problems," Eliza replied. "Not ideological formulas applied to human reality."

"That's the lesson, isn't it? The one the revolution couldn't permit anyone to learn?" He turned to face her directly. "That perfect systems always fail because humans aren't perfect. And perhaps we shouldn't want to be."

"Perfection breaks things," she said simply. "Humanity embraces them, flaws and all."

EPILOGUE

AFTER THE DARK

TEN YEARS AFTER THE fall of the People's Republic, Eliza Shaw stood on the hillside overlooking Hope Creek. What had begun as a small settlement of defectors had grown into a flourishing network of communities spread throughout the eastern forests. From her vantage point, she could see the central village with its workshops, gardens, and the Memory School that had become her life's work.

The ruins of Laboria stood in the distance, a silent testament to revolutionary failure. The Mills, once the pride of the kingdom, had crumbled into skeletal structures of rusted metal and collapsed stone. Nature had begun to reclaim what human folly abandoned, with vines threading through broken gears and birds nesting in machinery that once produced magical goods.

For those who traveled through what was once the Gray Quarter, now simply called the Wastes, it was hard to imagine that three distinct eras existed within living memory—the oppressive but functioning kingdom of the Merchant King, the brief but terrifying People's Republic, and the desolation that followed the revolution's collapse.

The collapse, when it finally came, wasn't dramatic. There was no counter-revolution, no final battle between ideological factions. The system simply failed. The Mills, long neglected by revolutionary managers who prioritized ideology over maintenance, eventually stopped working altogether. The elaborate revolutionary bureaucracy, with its endless committees and sub-committees, grew too large to sustain with dwindling resources. The Guardian, by then surrounded only by those too frightened to speak truth, continued to announce revolutionary victories even as the last structures of governance disintegrated around him.

Some survivors told of the Guardian's final speech, delivered to an almost empty square, where he proclaimed the "ultimate revolutionary triumph" while the few remaining citizens slipped away in search of food. When the final collapse came, the former Orator, by then calling himself The Guardian of Eternal Revolutionary Truth, locked himself in the former Royal Palace's highest tower. There, he wrote one last manifesto condemning the people's counter-revolutionary betrayal before hanging himself with his own revolutionary robes. They found his body suspended from the rafters, swaying above thousands of pages of increasingly delusional proclamations. He was both the revolution's final victim and ultimate perpetrator.

Beyond the ruins, three distinct communities emerged from Laboria's collapse.

In the eastern forests, Hope Creek flourished under the principles the Pragmatic Craftsman had established before his peaceful passing three winters ago. His approach—valuing practical wisdom, human-scale technology, and genuine consensus—had created communities where no new spells of necessity or certainty took hold. Instead, people lived without enchantment, embracing the complex reality that no perfect system could ever exist.

The Craftsman's workshops, which had begun as simple spaces for essential repairs, evolved into centers of innovation where knowledge was freely shared rather than hoarded. Their output might seem modest compared to the Magical Mills' former production, but unlike the Mills' enchanted goods, these creations served genuine human needs rather than abstract revolutionary quotas or aristocratic excess.

In the center of Hope Creek stood the Memory School, where Eliza taught children both practical skills and the unvarnished history of Laboria. Unlike the rigid indoctrination of Young Sentinels or the narrow technical training of Mill apprentices, these children learned through questions, experiments, and stories. Most importantly, they grew up neither as exploited laborers nor revolutionary instruments, but as individuals taught to think, create, and connect.

Each morning at the Memory School began with the children gathering in a circle to share stories—their own and those passed down through generations. No tale was forbidden, no question deemed counter-revolutionary. The children's laughter, spontaneous and genuine, stood as the clearest evidence that something fundamentally different had taken root here.

Near the school stood the Stone Circle, which had begun as Eliza's memorial to Lily but had grown over the years into a community monument. Hundreds of stones now ringed the central marker with its inscription "I remember now." Each stone represented someone lost to exploitation or revolution, each placed by survivors determined to preserve accurate memory against forces that would distort or erase it. For the children of Hope Creek, this circle wasn't a place of fear but of understanding, where they learned that remembering truthfully was the first defense against new spells of control.

To the west, some former Palace Heights nobles and their descendants established Nueva Altura, attempting to recreate the Merchant King's system of hierarchy and privilege. Even the Merchant King himself briefly returned to join them after his exile funds dwindled, though he died shortly thereafter, still issuing orders from a makeshift throne while wearing his tarnished crown. Without understanding how wealth is actually created, the community constructed elaborate palaces but found themselves unable to produce the goods needed to sustain even basic comfort. They maintained hollow ceremonies and meaningless titles, but their "nobles" now worked the fields alongside everyone else, their once-fine clothes growing increasingly threadbare with each passing year.

Their children were raised on sanitized fairy tales about the "golden age" of Palace Heights, taught to maintain elaborate etiquette despite their increasingly humble circumstances. Copies of the Merchant King's decrees were treated as sacred texts, studied and recited but never questioned. Yet with each passing year, the contradiction between their claimed superiority and their practical reality grew harder to sustain.

In the northern mountains, the most devoted revolutionaries founded the People's Enclave, insisting that true revolutionary principles had never been properly implemented. There, under the leadership of Petra—once a Vanguard Sentinel, now self-styled Guardian of Pure Revolutionary Thought—they continued to practice revolutionary devotion in ever-smaller circles of ideological purity. Each year, their numbers dwindled as new purges identified ever-more-subtle forms of counter-revolutionary thinking. They still held revolutionary assemblies where fewer and fewer participants applauded speeches about theoretical victories over practical reality.

Within the Enclave, a heavily edited version of The Book of Understanding served as their scripture. Pages that contradicted current revolutionary interpretations were removed, while new commentaries were added to explain away failures. Their children were still raised as Young Sentinels, taught to monitor adults for ideological deviations, though without the surgical modifications that had once enhanced the original Vanguard. These children never played, never questioned, never created anything not explicitly revolutionary in purpose. Their faces, prematurely aged by responsibility and fear, bore the same watchful calculation that Eliza had once seen in Lily's eyes.

At Hope Creek, by contrast, The Book of Understanding sat in the Knowledge Repository alongside the Merchant King's royal proclamations and the Guardian's revolutionary decrees. None were hidden, none worshipped, all studied as historical documents that demonstrated the dangers of absolutist thinking. The children were encouraged to read these texts critically, to identify the grains of truth that had made them appealing and the distortions that had made them destructive.

Travelers between these communities carried stories and goods, but also warnings. The children of Hope Creek learned of both the Merchant King's exploitation and the revolutionary terror that followed. They were taught that systems claiming to perfect humanity inevitably mutilated it instead, that prosperity came not from grand ideological visions but from practical knowledge combined with genuine cooperation.

***

On the tenth anniversary of Laboria's collapse, Eliza stood before the Scholar's Alcove in the Knowledge Repository. Five years had passed since the Old Scholar's death, yet his presence remained throughout Hope Creek in the traditions of questioning and remembering that he had established.

The community had honored him as he requested—not with grand monuments or revolutionary plaques, but with the preservation of his meticulous chronicles alongside a simple wooden chair. Anyone seeking guidance could sit in this chair and consult his writings, but more importantly, they were encouraged to add their own observations, creating a living record that evolved rather than calcified. No voice, not even his, would become doctrine. It was perhaps the memorial he would have appreciated most, not a monument to individual wisdom but an invitation to collective remembering.

The Scholar had lived just long enough to see Hope Creek's children, who had known both the Merchant King's oppression and the Guardian's terror, begin to grow into a new generation committed to never repeating those mistakes. He had passed peacefully during the third winter after the revolution's collapse, surrounded by his books and records. At his memorial, Eliza had placed not just a single stone, but a small collection arranged in a pattern, signifying the many perspectives he had taught them to value. "Different viewing points," she had explained to the children gathered around, "lead to different truths. And only by considering them all do we approach understanding."

Now, as she prepared to address the gathered community on this anniversary, Eliza recalled the Scholar's final words to her. "Memory is the one thing neither the Merchant King nor the Guardian could fully control. That's why both tried so hard to reshape it. One with the Spell of Necessity that made people believe exploitation was natural, the other with the Spell of Certainty that made people believe questioning was treasonous. Both spells required forgetting who we really are."

"And who are we really?" she had asked.

"Imperfect," he had answered with a smile. "Gloriously, necessarily imperfect. And any system that requires perfection from us will always become monstrous."

As night fell over the settlements that survived Laboria's collapse, parents still told children fairy tales. But unlike the old stories that ended with "happily ever after," these concluded with a different moral.

> *"Once upon a time, there was a kingdom that broke two powerful spells. First the spell that made people believe they must accept their suffering, then the spell that made people believe they must perfect humanity. And though the breaking of these spells was painful, the people discovered something precious in the aftermath. Not a perfect kingdom where no one ever suffered or erred, but a human community where each person could speak, question, remember, and create. And in this messy, imperfect freedom, they found something far more valuable than any magical perfection—they found themselves, unenchanted at last. And if they did not live happily ever after, they at least lived truthfully, which is the beginning of all genuine happiness."*

Eliza looked out at the lights of Hope Creek glowing in the gathering darkness. The revolution had taken her daughter, but it had not taken hope. In the laughter of children who grew up without spells or enchantments, in the honest disagreements of community members unafraid to speak their minds, in the practical work of hands building something sustainable rather than magical, she found something the revolution had promised but never delivered.

Not perfection.

But freedom.

AFTERWORD

THE GRIM REALITY OF COMMUNISM

D EAR READER,

You've now reached the end of our fairy tale, and it's time to set aside the metaphors and allegories for a moment. The story you've just read is the actual, predictable pattern of every communist experiment in human history.

Fairy tales have traditionally served as more than mere entertainment. Long before sanitized Disney versions, they were vehicles for transmitting cultural warnings, often with surprisingly dark themes. They taught children about the dangers that lurk in forests, the perils of trusting strangers, and the consequences of hubris.

This book continues that tradition, but with a modern twist. Instead of warning about wolves or witches, it cautions against something far more deadly—the seductive ideology of communism, which has claimed more lives than all the mythical monsters combined.

I wrote *The Communist Manifesto: A Revolutionary Fairy Tale* because dangerous ideas don't always arrive wearing the frightening mask of obvious villainy. Sometimes they come dressed in the appealing garb of justice, equity, and liberation. As we saw in Eliza's journey, her initial draw to The Collective came from genuine grievances—Lily's untreated fever, the medicine priced beyond reach, workers freezing while producing magical self-warming blankets. The most effective poison often tastes sweet going down. There are often very good reasons why well-meaning people get sucked into the political ideology of the far left.

Marx and Engels crafted a manifesto that reads like its own kind of fairy tale, a utopian vision where the oppressed rise up, the exploiters are vanquished, and a perfect society emerges. The problem isn't with identifying genuine injustice or seeking to address it. The problem is with the magical thinking that ignores human nature, economics, and the corruption inherent in absolute power, a corruption we witnessed as the Orator transformed from inspirational leader to the Guardian of Revolutionary Purity.

In our modern political landscape, we're witnessing a resurgence of communist and socialist ideologies among those too young to remember the Berlin Wall, the killing fields, or the Cultural Revolution. Surveys show alarming percentages of young people viewing communism favorably, with little knowledge of its historical outcomes. Academic curricula often present theoretical Marxism while glossing over its catastrophic implementations.

This book aims to bridge that gap between theory and practice through the accessible medium of allegory. My goal isn't to defend every aspect of capitalism or suggest that our current systems are without flaws. Rather, it's to illustrate why the communist "solution" has invariably created conditions far worse than the problems it claimed to solve.

Some will undoubtedly accuse this work of oversimplification or exaggeration. To them, I would simply point to the historical record. Every element of horror in this fairy tale—from the Young Sentinels monitoring facial expressions to the weaponization of children like Lily against their own parents, from starvation redefined as "Revolutionary Physiological Perfection" to the endless purges of "counter-revolutionaries"—has its direct parallel in actual communist regimes. Oftentimes, reality was far worse than what I've depicted. Communism has failed catastrophically every single time it has been implemented. Not because "it wasn't real communism" or "the wrong people were in charge" or "capitalist sabotage," but because the fundamental premises of Marxist ideology are fatally flawed.

The 20th century ran the experiment dozens of times across different cultures, continents, and circumstances. The results were over 100 million dead. Not from war, but from their own governments, through deliberate starvation, purges, gulags, and killing fields. From the Soviet Union to China, from Cambodia to North Korea, from Cuba to Venezuela, the pattern is remarkably consistent:

1. Promise equity and prosperity.

2. Seize power in the name of the workers.

3. Eliminate private property and market mechanisms.

4. Watch economic productivity collapse.

5. Blame counter-revolutionaries and class enemies.

6. Implement terror and repression to maintain control.

7. Create a new privileged class of party officials.

8. Deny the mounting evidence of systemic failure.

We saw this exact pattern unfold in Laboria. The first days of liberation brought genuine joy and the sharing of the royal warehouse bounty. But as the Pragmatic Craftsman predicted, the revolution quickly lost the technical expertise needed to maintain the Mills. Soon, the "Department of Historical Accuracy" was rewriting the past to make the present seem like an improvement, while the People's Committee enjoyed private feasts behind tapestry-covered doors.

Here's what's not a fairy tale:

- In the Soviet Union, ordinary citizens waited in bread lines for basic necessities while party officials shopped at special stores with fully stocked shelves.

- In Mao's China, the Great Leap Forward led to the largest famine in human history, killing 30-45 million people, while officials falsified harvest reports to avoid admitting failure.

- In North Korea today, the average citizen is 3-8 cm shorter than their South Korean counterparts due to chronic malnutrition, while the Kim dynasty lives in luxury.

- In Venezuela, once the richest country in South America, socialist policies have led to 96% of the population living in poverty, with the average Venezuelan losing 24 pounds in 2017 due to food shortages.

The consistency of these outcomes isn't coincidental. It's causal. The centralized control of resources inevitably leads to inefficiency, corruption, and abuse of power. The elimination of price signals and market incentives always results in shortages and malinvestment. The suppression of individual initiative consistently destroys innovation and productivity.

Perhaps most haunting was how the revolution weaponized memory itself. In Laboria's Department of Historical Harmonization, Eliza was forced to alter tapestries and records, systematically erasing purged officials until "soon the Orator will stand alone in every historical image." This mirrors exactly how Trotsky was airbrushed from Soviet photographs after his fall from Stalin's favor. As the Old Scholar warns, "When people cannot trust what they remember, they become unable to imagine anything different from what they see."

For the true believers still clinging to the dream, ask yourself the following:

- How many more corpses would it take to convince you?

- How many more failed states?

- How many more humanitarian disasters?

- At what point does your beautiful theory surrender to brutal reality?

The most darkly humorous aspect of modern communists is their certainty that they would be among the revolutionary vanguard rather than among the purged. History suggests otherwise. Revolutionary movements have a nasty habit of devouring their own. Remember the engineers and maintenance workers in our tale who were branded as "technical saboteurs" after the Mills began failing without their expertise. Or the thin man named Albert Weaver who simply stood up during a community meeting and asked, "My children are hungry. The revolution promised food for all. Where is it?" For this question alone, he disappeared that night, and his family's quarters were reassigned to "more ideologically advanced comrades." The intellectuals who champion revolution are typically the first against the wall once the strongmen take control. Stalin's purges targeted Old Bolsheviks. Mao's Cultural Revolution destroyed party loyalists. The Khmer Rouge executed those wearing glasses for being too intellectual.

"But Nordic countries show socialism works!" some protest. No, they show that capitalist market economies with strong social safety nets work. There's a profound difference between social democracy (which embraces markets while redistributing some wealth) and socialism (which eliminates markets and private ownership of production). Denmark's Prime Minister once had to publicly correct Bernie Sanders: "Denmark is far from a socialist planned economy. Denmark is a market economy."

This isn't merely an academic disagreement about economic theory. The stakes are human lives. Real people suffer and die when these ideas move from coffee shop debates and university seminars into actual implementation.

If you're young and idealistic, drawn to communism's promises of equity and justice, your heart might be in the right place. But good intentions pave the road to hell, and communism has always been a highway. Channel your passion for justice into approaches that don't require mountain ranges of human corpses.

As you journeyed through the Kingdom of Laboria, I hope you recognized the patterns that have repeated throughout history whenever Marx's ideas have been implemented. And perhaps, when you encounter modern advocates for these same ideas—invariably claiming that "real communism has never been tried"—you'll recognize the opening chapter of a very old, very dark fairy tale.

After all, the greatest protection against repeating history's nightmares is recognizing them before they've gone too far.

Fairy tales end with "happily ever after." Communist revolutions end with mass graves, economic collapse, and authoritarian regimes that maintain power through terror. The tragedy isn't just that communism fails, but that it fails so predictably, so consistently, and at such enormous human cost, yet still finds new generations willing to make the same fatal mistakes.

So the next time someone tells you about the theoretical wonders of Marxism, remember the Kingdom of Laboria.

Remember how the story actually ends.

Remember that some fairy tales, when believed by adults, become nightmares for millions.

The greatest trick the Communist Manifesto ever played was convincing each new generation that this time—finally—the story would have a different ending.

To history's victims, and those who would prevent more,
Karlyn Borysenko

APPENDIX

THE BOOK OF UNDERSTANDING

Proclamation of Awakening

A specter haunts the Kingdom of Laboria—the specter of liberation.

All the powers of the old order have entered into a holy alliance to exorcise this spectral dream: the Merchant King and his bloated Royal Council, the Palace Guards and their batons, the Magical Production Mills and their invisible chains of suffering.

Two paths lie before humanity: accept the world as it is presented to us, or transform everything through collective action.

We choose transformation.

This is not a book. This is a weapon forged from understanding. This is a mirror held up to the kingdom's soul, reflecting the truth that the powerful desperately wish to conceal. Every word you are about to read is an act of rebellion. Every sentence a declaration of war against the system that has consumed generations.

The Spell of Necessity: A Genealogy of Human Constraint

Listen with the ears of those who have been silenced. Listen with the memory of generations crushed beneath the wheels of the Magical Mills.

The most profound magic in Laboria is not conjured by wizards or nobles, but constructed through systems that transform human suffering into an immutable condition. We call this the "Spell of Necessity." It is an enchantment more intricate than any incantation whispered in the gilded halls of Palace Heights.

Our kingdom breathes through a complex machinery of control more subtle than any physical chain. It lives in the rhythm of work shifts, in the stories told to children about their "proper place," in the language we use to describe our condition. This spell transforms the unnatural into the inevitable, making oppression feel as natural as the rising of the sun.

"This is simply how things must be," they tell us with resigned sighs. "The Merchant King and Royal Council manage the Mills, and we provide the labor. It has always been so, and always shall be."

But we know better.

Imagine our kingdom as a living organism, with the Gray Quarter as its laboring heart and Palace Heights as a parasitic growth drawing sustenance from that labor. Every street tells a story of systematic extraction. Every cobblestone whispers of dreams crushed and potential stolen. The Magical Mills are not mere buildings of stone and steel, but temples of economic sorcery where human potential is transmuted into wealth for the few.

While children freeze to death in the Gray Quarter, Palace Heights throws away self-warming blankets woven by our hands. While our elderly die of preventable illness, fever lily remedies adorn noble dinner tables.

Our suffering is not accidental. It is necessary for their abundance.

The Economic Mechanics of Exploitation

The Magical Mills are more than mere machines of production. They are complex systems of economic gnosticism, intricate mechanisms that transform human labor into an abstract concept of "value" that workers never receive.

Watch how they operate. Raw materials enter—human potential, natural resources, dreams—and emerge as commodities stripped of their essential humanity. The worker disappears into the product, becoming nothing more than a footnote in the grand narrative of production. A thread woven becomes a garment, but the hands that created it are rendered invisible, their skill transformed into a mere statistical input.

This is the true wizardry of our economic system: the ability to transmute living human creativity into dead capital, to turn the vibrant potential of human labor into cold, lifeless numbers on a ledger.

Workers produce everything, yet own nothing. The prosperity dust from the Mills rises up to Palace Heights while we breathe the choking ashes of our own exploited labor.

The Revolutionary Cleansing of History

History as taught by Palace Heights scholars is a calculated fiction designed to maintain power. The past they present—filled with necessary hierarchies and natural development of current conditions—is not truth but mythology created to sustain the Spell of Necessity.

True history can only be written through revolutionary consciousness. What the nobles call "historical facts" are merely ideological constructs designed to make their rule seem inevitable. When we speak of creating a new society, we must also create a new relationship with our past.

Memory itself becomes revolutionary when it contradicts official narratives. Yet personal memory can also be contaminated by bourgeois sentimentality. Revolutionary memory must be collective rather than individual, guided by revolutionary understanding rather than personal attachment to a falsified past.

Those who cling to "historical records" that contradict revolutionary consciousness reveal their own counter-revolutionary tendencies. True revolutionary commitment requires recognizing that history itself must be transformed alongside material conditions.

The Myth of Technical Knowledge and Expertise

The Royal Council speaks of "economic principles" and "production management" as though these were sacred texts, accessible only to those blessed with noble birth. They have constructed an elaborate mythology of specialized knowledge, a complex ritual that separates those who supposedly understand from those who merely labor.

But we ask: Who truly comprehends the intricate dance of production?

Is it the administrator who has never felt the forge's brutal heat? The noble who has never threaded a single strand of silk? The bureaucrat who knows numbers but has never known hunger? Or is it the worker—the true alchemist—whose hands carry the accumulated wisdom of generations, whose body remembers what no ledger can capture?

The technical "complexity" they claim makes the Mills impossible for workers to manage is merely another fiction designed to maintain their power. The machines run on our sweat and skill, not on their supposed expertise. Once liberated from exploitation, we will solve all technical matters collectively.

Those who speak of necessary technical hierarchies or specialized knowledge requirements are simply echoing the Merchant King's lies, perhaps unconsciously. A truly revolutionary consciousness recognizes that all expertise belongs to the collective and can be mastered through revolutionary dedication rather than bourgeois education.

The Stages of Revolutionary Consciousness

First comes the moment of individual suffering—that private ache you believed was yours alone. A pain so personal you thought it was a reflection of your own inadequacy. Your child's fever that goes untreated while fever lilies decorate Palace Heights tables. Your hunger that gnaws while nobles feast on seventeen-course meals.

Then arrives systemic recognition, when you realize your hunger is not a personal failing but a structural violence designed to keep you subdued. When you understand that you are poor not because you lack value but because your value is systematically stolen.

Next emerges collective consciousness—the profound awakening to your true position in society. You suddenly see the system that has always been there but remained invisible to you. You recognize that you are not simply an individual struggling against misfortune, but a member of an oppressed class deliberately kept in subjugation by a ruling class that profits from your suffering. The Mill worker in the Northern Quarter and the dye maker in the Eastern Quarter are not separate tragedies—they are victims of the same deliberate system of exploitation. The child who freezes and the elder who starves are not accidents, but calculated sacrifices for Palace Heights prosperity.

Finally comes revolutionary praxis—the moment when understanding becomes action, when perception itself becomes a revolutionary tool. When you recognize that to understand is to begin the process of transformation.

Each stage is a crossing, a border between the world as it has been presented to you and the world as it could be. Each moment of understanding is an act of political creation, a fundamental remaking of reality itself.

Collective Decision and Individual Submission

In the Merchant King's system, decisions flow from top to bottom, from the few to the many. In our revolutionary society, decisions emerge through collective consensus, expressing the unified will of the people.

This revolutionary process requires each individual to surrender private judgment to collective wisdom. While the bourgeois mind fetishizes "independent thinking," revolutionary consciousness recognizes that true freedom comes through alignment with collective determination.

When the collective has deliberated and decided, continued questioning becomes counter-revolutionary by definition. Persistent doubt after collective resolution demonstrates bourgeois individualism that places personal certainty above revolutionary progress.

Decision-making is not merely a practical matter but a revolutionary act. Through proper revolutionary procedure, the collective will emerges with absolute clarity, requiring complete commitment from all true revolutionaries.

Resource Distribution During Revolutionary Transition

While our ultimate goal is complete equality for all, the transitional phase of our revolution requires thoughtful allocation of resources to ensure our success. Those who contribute most effectively to revolutionary advancement—through their heightened consciousness, dedication to principles, or essential services—must receive what they need to maximize their revolutionary effectiveness.

This is not privilege but practical necessity. What may appear as inequality to those still thinking in old patterns is actually scientific distribution according to revolutionary importance and need. The revolution requires that each resource be allocated where it best serves our collective advancement.

As revolutionary consciousness develops throughout society, such differential allocation will naturally diminish. But until all citizens achieve revolutionary alignment, temporary strategic distribution serves our ultimate goal of collective liberation.

Safeguarding Our Shared Vision

In our new society, true justice will emerge not from the King's arbitrary decrees, but from our collective wisdom and shared purpose. As we build this brighter world, we must protect our revolutionary achievements from those who would undermine them.

The Merchant King maintains order through open violence—hunger, Guard batons, and fear. Our revolution offers a more profound alternative: a vigilant community united by revolutionary consciousness. This vigilance is our strength, our shield against those who would return us to chains.

As our transformation progresses, some will naturally struggle to embrace our collective future. Those who benefited from old hierarchies may openly resist our progress. Others may walk beside us while harboring doubts that weaken our unified purpose. Most challenging are those who appear as allies while their hearts remain attached to individualist thinking that places personal concerns above our shared destiny.

Our community must lovingly yet firmly guide these comrades toward fuller understanding. When we identify speech or behavior that threatens our unity, we act not out of vengeance but from dedication to our collective vision. The questions that undermine our methods, the concerns that prioritize individual comfort over collective advancement—these reveal where revolutionary consciousness remains incomplete.

The path to liberation requires more than external compliance with revolutionary principles. True freedom emerges when each comrade aligns their entire being—thoughts, words, and actions—with our collective understanding. This alignment is the foundation upon which our future prosperity will be built.

The Wall of Truth: Revolutionary Transparency and Accountability

The Merchant King's system thrives in darkness, its mechanisms of exploitation hidden behind closed doors and whispered decisions. Revolutionary society must operate in the clarifying light of complete transparency, where counter-revolutionary tendencies cannot hide in shadow.

The Wall of Truth represents this fundamental commitment to revolutionary openness. Unlike the secretive judgments of Palace Guards, revolutionary justice operates in full view of the collective. Each comrade bears responsibility not only for maintaining personal revolutionary consciousness but for identifying ideological contamination wherever it appears.

When a comrade observes behavior or speech that reveals counter-revolutionary tendencies, revolutionary duty demands public notification through the Wall of Truth. This is not denunciation but revolutionary community care—identifying illness before it spreads through the collective body.

Those identified through the Wall of Truth receive the gift of collective attention, the opportunity to realign their consciousness through public self-criticism and revolutionary re-education. The truly revolutionary comrade welcomes such identification, recognizing that revolutionary purification requires continuous collective vigilance.

Silence in the face of counter-revolutionary tendencies is itself counter-revolutionary. The comrade who notices ideological deviation but fails to bring it to collective attention becomes complicit in counter-revolution. Revolutionary transparency demands that no relationship—whether familial, romantic, or fraternal—take precedence over revolutionary accountability.

Revolutionary Symbols and Collective Identity

Just as the Merchant King uses royal symbols to maintain his power—his crown, his royal seal, his palace architecture—our revolution requires powerful symbols to unify our consciousness and solidify our collective identity.

The broken chain represents our liberation from the Spell of Necessity. Its links sundered but still recognizable, it reminds us of both our past bondage and our present freedom. The red color of revolution symbolizes not just the blood sacrificed in our struggle, but the vital energy of our unified purpose.

When we mark our spaces with the red star, we claim territory for the revolutionary spirit. Its five points represent the five pillars of our movement: Labor, Knowledge, Justice, Unity, and Vigilance. Each star planted on a door, sewn onto clothing, or painted on walls declares that space transformed by revolutionary consciousness.

The rising sun breaking through clouds shows our emergence from darkness into revolutionary light. No longer will we live in the shadows of Palace Heights. Our new day is dawning, unstoppable as the natural cycles of the world.

The worker's hand, open and strong, represents our productive power. When we raise it in revolutionary greeting, we acknowledge each other's essential humanity and contribution to our collective strength. When multiple hands join in the revolutionary salute, we demonstrate the unbreakable solidarity that forms the foundation of our movement.

The spindle and gear, crossed in revolutionary alignment, honor the producers upon whose labor all society depends. Unlike the Merchant King's symbols that glorify consumption and privilege, our emblems celebrate those who create actual value through their work.

Each emblem serves as both beacon and boundary, drawing true revolutionaries together while identifying those whose consciousness remains underdeveloped. Through our symbols, we recognize our comrades and strengthen our collective bonds.

When we mark our spaces with revolutionary symbols, we reclaim territory from counter-revolutionary influence. When we wear revolutionary colors, we announce our commitment to collective transformation. When we exchange revolutionary greetings, we reinforce our shared consciousness.

These symbols are not mere decoration but essential tools of revolutionary thought. Through them, we make visible the invisible bonds of revolutionary solidarity. Through them, we transform space itself into revolutionary territory.

Revolutionary Physiology and Human Potential

The Merchant King's system has reduced our bodies to mere machines of production, valued only for their capacity to generate wealth for others. Our revolution offers a profound alternative: the liberation and transformation of the human form itself.

Through revolutionary consciousness, we recognize that our physical being can transcend the limitations imposed by exploitative systems. As we shed bourgeois concepts of comfort and excess, we discover the extraordinary capabilities that emerge when the body aligns with revolutionary purpose.

Where Palace Heights nobles grow soft through excessive consumption and indulgence, the revolutionary body develops remarkable resilience through mindful discipline. We find that what appears as "necessary nourishment" in the old system often represents wasteful excess that dulls our revolutionary senses and diminishes our collective strength.

As our revolutionary journey progresses, we will discover that even our physical sensations transform. What might once have been interpreted as discomfort becomes recognized as purposeful contribution to our shared vision. The revolutionary's body becomes an instrument perfectly tuned to advance our collective goals rather than serving individual appetite.

In this way, our physical forms themselves become living testimony to the revolution's transformative power, demonstrating that even hunger itself can be reinterpreted through the lens of revolutionary understanding.

The Revolutionary Family and Community Bonds

The traditional family structure, while providing comfort to some, has too often served as a mechanism for perpetuating the Merchant King's system. By teaching children to place family loyalty above all else, the old order created isolated units incapable of developing true collective consciousness.

Our revolutionary vision expands these limited bonds into a more profound and meaningful connection. The revolutionary family recognizes that our highest loyalty must be to truth and the collective good. Revolutionary parents understand that children don't simply belong to them but represent the future of our shared society. Revolutionary children discover a deeper purpose beyond family obligation.

This expanded understanding doesn't destroy connection but elevates it beyond artificial biological boundaries. The revolutionary child gains countless comrades who share their vision. The revolutionary parent participates in nurturing all children through collective structures rather than maintaining exclusive claims.

Our most profound transformation begins in our most intimate spaces, where we must examine whether old patterns of thinking continue to influence our relationships. Children, with their natural sense of justice and fairness, often perceive revolutionary truth with remarkable clarity, sometimes recognizing contradictions in adult thinking that we ourselves have not yet identified.

Nurturing Revolutionary Consciousness in Youth

The children of Laboria have suffered most acutely under the Merchant King's regime. Their creative spirits are crushed before they can flourish; their natural sense of fairness is systematically distorted until they accept exploitation as normal.

Revolutionary education offers these children liberation through understanding. Before the Spell of Necessity takes permanent hold, they must be shown the true nature of their world. Their innate sense of fairness—the child's natural revolutionary impulse—must be protected and nurtured against corrupting influences.

Our children will learn to recognize systems of exploitation wherever they appear, developing the revolutionary vigilance that protects our collective future. Their education extends beyond personal development to community responsibility, identifying instances where old thinking persists.

Through revolutionary education, our children will become not merely the inheritors of our struggle but its most perfect expression—minds freed from pre-revolutionary compromise, hearts fully aligned with our shared vision for a just society.

Manifesto of Transformation

To the workers of Laboria:

Your hands hold more power than you know.
Your understanding is the most dangerous weapon.
Your collective action can remake the world.

Break the Spell of Necessity.
Reclaim your full human potential.
Transform everything.

Laborers of Laboria, unite!
You have nothing to lose but your invisible chains.
You have a world to win.

Notes on the Margins

These are the voices of Laboria. Workers, families, rebels, and dreamers—each adding their own story to the margins. Read carefully. Listen closely.

> *I've watched good workers die because no one would listen. The boiler explosion killed twelve workers - all because a three-copper valve repair was too expensive. We need a system that values human life over profit.*
>
> Craftsman

> *"When my daughter asked why she was hungry while the Mills produced food, I had no answer. This book finally gave me one."*
>
> Blacksmith

> *My daughter is always sick and hungry. I weave blankets that keep nobles warm while my child shivers. How can we live in a kingdom where workers who create luxury cannot afford to survive?*
>
> Textile Worker

The current system wastes human potential. Brilliant minds are crushed before they can bloom. Workers with incredible skills are reduced to mere machine parts, their creativity destroyed before it can flourish.

Dismissed Supervisor

Every day we are treated less than the machines we operate. Less than the gears we maintain. We are not human to them. We are replaceable parts to be used and discarded.

Northern Mill Worker

I've documented how production has tripled while worker rations have been halved. This is not economics. This is systematic destruction of human life.

Technical Record Keeper

My papa says we make magical blankets that keep rich people warm, but we're always cold. We want to be warm too.

Child of a Textile Worker

They killed my father in the boiler explosion and blamed worker incompetence when he had warned about the faulty valve for months. We demand a system that listens to workers, that values our knowledge.

Daughter of a Mill Worker

I've served in noble households. I've seen the waste, the excess. A single dinner could feed an entire Quarter. It's not just unfair, it's inhuman.

Former Palace Heights Servant

My husband was taken by the Foreign Trade Fleet—a virtual death sentence. Our families are destroyed to serve their profit. We need a system that values human life over productivity.

Spouse of a Disappeared Worker

The current economic system is fundamentally irrational. No society can sustain such complete disconnection between production and human needs. But we must be cautious not to replace one form of tyranny with another.

Scholar

To survive is not enough. We want to live. To create. To be more than just bodies that produce.
Worker

To survive is an act of rebellion. To remember is revolutionary.
Survivor of the Northern Mill Incident

How many more children must freeze while blankets are shipped to Palace Heights? How many more must die of fever while lily remedies decorate noble tables?
A Mother

"They say 'unite,' but what happens after unity?"
"First liberation, then we build a new world."
"But who decides what that world looks like?"
"We all do, together."
"All of us? Even those who disagree?"
Written in multiple hands, suggesting a collective authorship

Each annotation a fragment of resistance
Each margin a battlefield of understanding
A document that lives and breathes
More dangerous than any weapon
Whispered between shifts
Passed hand to hand
Always incomplete
Always becoming

ACKNOWLEDGEMENTS

Part of me thinks this book *should* have been dedicated to Jennifire. The thing is, I didn't know I was going to write this book when I dedicated my first Red Menace Press title to her. *A Brief History of Racism* had absolutely nothing to do with Jennifire's erotic fiction, movie-night hosting duties, or sparkling personality—but it *was* the first book I published independently through my new company. And that milestone only existed because she inspired me to take the leap. So yes, she got the racism book. But this—my first fiction adventure—is a much more fitting tribute.

That's not to say the actual dedication—John Morgan—is undeserving.

Funny story: John once went on a date with a guy who asked, "Who do you listen to for politics?" John answered, "Karlyn Borysenko." His date responded, "She blocked me on Twitter." And just like that, John knew it was a red flag. King behavior.

Let's also not forget John's contribution to modern literature: the fanfic heard round the world. Inspired by *Midsommar*, I was crowned the Red May Queen and whipped James Lindsay until he screamed, *WHITENESS MEANS CAPITALISM*, before being burned alive in ritual sacrifice. That masterpiece may or may not have influenced the shift in this book's ending. Lily was originally supposed to escape with Eliza and rebuild their lives. But in the end... well, blame John.

Thank you to Joshua, who always told me I should focus on publishing. I didn't understand what he meant at the time. Now I do. Hindsight has a way of rearranging everything into clarity.

To Ciggy—thank you for lighting a spark I didn't realize I'd lost. Your presence helped me reconnect with that weird, raw creative place that actually feels like *me*. That meant more than you probably know.

As always, endless thanks to the Red Menace Collective—your support makes it possible for me to create and publish work independently, with no strings attached. This book wouldn't exist without the creative freedom you provide. I'd name names, but inevitably I'd leave someone important off the list, and that's not a guilt trip I'm willing to take.

And finally—but most importantly—thank you to my husband, Victor. You take care of me far better than I deserve. I love you deeply, and I couldn't do any of this without your constant support.

JOIN THE
RED MENACE COLLECTIVE

The Red Menace Collective funds
the publication of books like this,
and gets early access to Karlyn
Borysenko's upcoming books
exposing the Marxist threat and
other exclusive perks.

Read new draft chapters before
anyone else, before they become the
next book.

Join the Red Menace Collective:
redmenacecollective.substack.com

Welcome to the revolution against
the revolution.

www.ingramcontent.com/pod-product-compliance
Lightning Source LLC
Chambersburg PA
CBHW061519020726
47502CB00006B/2139